"It's my mother."

Candy continued. "One of your—" she sought for an appropriate word, knowing scandal sheets wouldn't do "—papers has got a story about her. My—my father is..." She found she could not go on.

"And you were going to offer me a bargain, so the paper wouldn't print the story."

Candy flushed. "It sounds bad, put like that."

"What were you going to offer?"

"You wouldn't settle for my undying gratitude, I suppose?" she said, trying for a lightness she didn't feel.

"That would depend on how it was expressed."

There was a long silence in which Candy felt as if she were being slowly stretched until she snapped.

"I don't believe you said that. Do you think you're some kind of movie mogul with a casting couch?"

Justin seemed amused. "I was thinking of marriage."

Sophie Weston wrote and illustrated her first book at the age of five. After university she decided on a career in international finance, which was tremendously stimulating and demanding, but it was not enough. Something was missing in her life, and that something turned out to be writing. These days her life is complete. She loves exciting travel and adventures, yet hates to stray too long from her homey cottage in Chelsea, where she writes.

Books by Sophie Weston

HARLEQUIN ROMANCE

1925—BEWARE THE HUNTSMAN
2005—GOBLIN COURT
2129—WIFE TO CHARLES
2218—UNEXPECTED HAZARD
2362—AN UNDEFENDED CITY
3186—GYPSY IN THE NIGHT

HARLEQUIN PRESENTS

918—LIKE ENEMIES
942—SHADOW PRINCESS
957—YESTERDAY'S MIRROR
980—BEYOND RANSOM
1014—CHALLENGE
1246—A MATTER OF FEELING

NO PROVOCATION
Sophie Weston

Harlequin Books

TORONTO • NEW YORK • LONDON
AMSTERDAM • PARIS • SYDNEY • HAMBURG
STOCKHOLM • ATHENS • TOKYO • MILAN
MADRID • WARSAW • BUDAPEST • AUCKLAND

Original hardcover edition published in 1992
by Mills & Boon Limited

ISBN 0-373-03262-5

Harlequin Romance first edition April 1993

NO PROVOCATION

Printed in U.S.A.

CHAPTER ONE

CANDY NEILSON drew a deep breath. Someone was watching her.

Cautiously, she looked round her mother's drawing-room. Nobody met her eyes. Nobody seemed to be staring at her out of the crowd.

If only Dave had come with her. But when she had tried, shyly, to suggest it he had looked at her with blank incomprehension. Said she deserved an evening off. Said she would enjoy it, Candy remembered bitterly.

She smoothed the velvet skirt she was so reluctantly wearing. Sophisticated make-up disguised the pallor of her oval face. Her red hair was piled on the top of her head with deceptive casualness. Artless curling tendrils drifted against her cheek and the graceful length of her neck. She looked cool and poised and she knew it. She felt sick.

She could still feel those unseen eyes on her. She began to shake. After all this time, she thought despairingly, I ought to be able to walk into a cocktail party without collapsing. What's wrong with me?

Her mother saw her at once and came over, weaving expertly through the chattering groups. She too wore her make-up as if it were armour. Candy, who loved her, could see the strain in the lovely eyes.

'Darling, you're here. How nice.'

A scented cheek was pressed against her own.

'I said I would,' Candy said steadily.

Judith Neilson's eyes skidded away from hers. There had been a major fight about it, but Lady Neilson was not in the business of remembering battles when they were over.

'Have you seen your father?' she asked, looking round the room casually.

The groups were very nearly as tightly packed as a rush-hour underground train, Candy thought drily. The only difference was that they were drinking expensive alcohol and a good half of them were in dinner-jackets.

She said, 'It's not easy to see anyone in this crush.'

Even as she said it, she realised sharply that it wasn't true. Across the room a tall, dark man was watching her. Candy had no trouble in seeing him at all. In fact, as their eyes met, she realised that it was he watching her from the first.

He was tall and slim, with a fierce profile. Attraction blazed out of him like a death-ray. You could see it in the faces of the women round him, even though he was ignoring them.

The familiar shivery feeling she so despised began. But she would not let herself give in to it. She lifted her chin and glared straight back at him. His eyebrows rose. He looked amused. The shivers got worse.

Beside her Judith was saying distractedly, 'He promised he'd come. He promised.'

She had never seen the stranger before, Candy thought positively. She would have remembered those laughing eyes. She tried and failed to tear her own away.

'He?' she said vaguely.

'Your father. Are you sure you haven't seen him?'

With an effort Candy brought her attention back to her mother.

'Pops? You mean he isn't here?'

That alone was enough to account for the strain. Though Judith was determinedly ignoring it, Candy knew that the fragile marriage was as rocky as she could remember.

She wondered briefly if all only children were in the same position. She felt like a small nation caught between two warring empires. She couldn't remember a time when she hadn't felt like that: tentative, careful, her every feeling policed in case it gave rise to a declaration of hostilities. What would it be like to be spontaneous? She sighed.

Judith said, 'I don't know.' In the crowded room she kept her voice level and her expression casual. But Candy could feel the panic fluttering just below the surface. 'He's in a strange mood. We had an argument last night. When you were out. I would have told you but you came in so late.'

She could not quite banish the note of reproach. Candy skirted it cautiously. At some point her parents were going to have to find out that she was working at the Homeless Centre. Her father was not at home often enough to notice, but her mother was beginning to complain about the hours she had started to keep. She would have to tell them. But she would choose her moment carefully.

And in her heart of hearts she still hoped that Dave Tresilian would be with her when she did. Though that was more a dream than a hope, and she knew it.

With or without Dave's support, however, she was not going to be able to break the unwelcome news about her future in the middle of a cocktail party.

So she said, 'What sort of argument?'

For the tiniest fraction of a second Judith looked sick. The expression was banished immediately.

'We can't talk about it now. He won't let me down. I'm sure he won't. He must have been held up at the office. This take-over,' she murmured. She gave a bright smile to a new arrival. 'Wonderful to see you. Get together later. Find yourself a drink.' She looked suddenly at Candy. 'Darling, you haven't got a drink either.'

She gestured at one of the hired waiters who was circulating with a tray of canapés. 'Would you fetch my daughter a glass of champagne, please?'

Candy didn't like champagne but she didn't protest. She knew there was no point. It was part of one's duty at a cocktail party to circulate carrying a glass. You could quite often get away without drinking from it, she had found.

Judith scanned the room. 'You'll talk to Megan, won't you? Her son's back from Brazil. And Tom Langton. You were a bit abrupt with him last week, darling...'

Across the room the tall stranger was still watching her, his expression quizzical. He was nominally part of a group gathered round a vivacious friend of Lady Neilson's. But he was not even pretending to listen to the lively conversation. As Candy watched, he left them without a word. He began to shoulder his way through the crowd on a steady course that would bring him to her side. He did not take his eyes off her.

'*Mother*,' Candy said urgently.

'Here's your drink, darling.' Judith took it from the waiter with her charming smile and pressed it into Candy's hand. 'There you are, darling, it'll make you feel livelier. You can look a bit *grim*, you know.'

'Mother, who's that man?' Candy demanded, unheeding.

Judith's brows rose at this unusual display of interest from her only child. Pleased, she turned.

'The Spellborough man? Or the American that Sally——' She broke off. All the careful social poise fell away from her like a dropped bath-towel, Candy thought, shocked at the sight. 'Oh, my God. What's he doing here?'

Judith was looking straight at the dark stranger. He had been intercepted by a plump matron with her hand on his chest. But there was no doubt at all that his progress was only temporarily delayed.

'Who is he?' said Candy.

'Drink your champagne. I must...' Judith was distracted.

'Who?'

Her mother sent her a harried glance.

'He's a man called Justin Richmond. He runs the Richmond group. Your father has regarded him as a personal sort of enemy ever since he poached that woman's editor from the *Gaze*—Lizbeth Lamont. And now your father and he—well, to be honest, darling, he's the man your father thinks is behind the resistance to his bid for Richmonds. He'll be *furious* if he gets here and finds Justin Richmond at my party.'

Candy whistled. 'Too right.'

It was a measure of Judith's agitation that she did not reprimand her.

Justin Richmond had detached himself, and was making straight towards them.

Judith looked at Candy sharply. 'Are you sure you don't know him?'

Candy shook her head. 'Never seen him before in my life.'

'Well, he seems to know you.'

Agitation flickered. Oh, if only Dave were here. She calmed herself deliberately.

'I know. He's been looking at me ever since I came in.'

Judith looked even more worried. 'What's he up to? If your father... We'll have to get rid of him *quickly*.'

But Justin Richmond had reached them.

'Lady Neilson,' he said, though he was looking at Candy.

His eyes, she saw, were a strange, deep colour, so it looked as if he was looking at you with his whole heart and mind. The impression of intensity was disturbing. It certainly seemed to unsettle Judith's practised poise.

'Mr Richmond. I didn't realise you...that is...'

'No, I'm not on your guest list,' he agreed, amused. 'Polly Davent asked me to bring her.'

Mrs Davent's husband had walked out on her in a spectacular scene at a nightclub just before Christmas. She was putting a brave face on it—and turning up to social occasions with a range of surprising escorts. She was also an old friend of Judith's. Candy looked at her mother curiously. It was a nice social dilemma.

Judith did not have time to react, however. The alarming man had already turned to Candy.

'We haven't met. I'm Justin Richmond.'

As if mesmerised, she put out her hand.

'Candida Neilson.'

For a moment his face went still, the strange eyes going flat as if he was looking inwards instead of out. Then he smiled, a small private smile that made Candy even more uneasy than she was already.

'Delighted,' he murmured.

She had the feeling he meant it—and for no kindly reason. She cast her mother a quick imploring look. It went unanswered.

Judith said swiftly, 'Darling, why don't you show Mr Richmond the picture gallery? I believe he's a collector, too.'

The dark eyes crinkled with amusement. 'Not in the same class as Sir Leslie,' he demurred.

But Judith, with one eye on the door for her husband's arrival, virtually hustled them out. 'Show him the Kokoschka your father's just bought,' she said. 'It's said to be one of his finest.' And under her breath she hissed in Candy's ear, 'Get rid of him, for God's sake.'

Candy was almost certain that Justin Richmond heard. Anyway, he couldn't be in much doubt about the effect his uninvited presence was having on her mother, she thought, horribly embarrassed. Not knowing what to say, she led the way to the gallery.

It was an L-shaped room under the roof that spanned the entire ground-plan of the house. Lights were on and refreshments set out in readiness for any of the guests who proved to be art-lovers. The room was unoccupied. Justin Richmond looked round.

'Impressive.'

He went over to a small painting in an alcove. His shoes clipped on the polished wooden floor. Candy cast desperately around for something to say. *Oh, Dave, why aren't you here?*

She cleared her throat. 'What do you collect, Mr Richmond?'

He swung neatly round to face her. 'Oh, I wouldn't say I collect,' he drawled. 'Not like this. I just sometimes see something special, something very beautiful. Or moving.'

His eyes on her were like a caress and yet not: like a collector running a possessive hand down one of his acquisitions, Candy thought. She remembered that feeling from when she'd walked into the drawing-room this evening. He must have been watching her even then. She wanted to turn and run.

Instead she found herself saying huskily, 'And when you do?'

He shrugged. But there was nothing casual about him. That strange intensity was still there, in the tall frame, the handsome face.

'Oh, then I go after it.'

To Candy, still off balance, it sounded like a warning. She stared at him, her brows flying up.

'Are you saying you're going after one of my father's pictures? Should I warn him?' she said, trying to sound amused.

Justin Richmond chuckled. 'Oh I think I can live without his *pictures*.'

Candy thought frantically. The take-over, of course. She had paid little attention to it and, since her refusal to go into his publishing empire, Sir Leslie had not discussed his business affairs at home.

She said slowly, 'I'm not sure what there is between you and my father.'

He gave a soft laugh. 'So far, nothing more than harsh words and bad blood.'

'So far?'

'I have a presentiment that things just changed.'

She was bewildered. 'I don't understand. I'm afraid I don't take much interest in business,' she said carefully.

He didn't answer her. Instead he subjected her to a long, thoughtful inspection which set her teeth on edge.

Then he said easily, 'That suits me fine.'

Candy's slow-burning fuse ignited. It was not often that she lost her temper. She could not remember having done it since she was six or seven. But there was something about this man—his ease, his amusement, above all that intent, intense study of her ever since she arrived at the party—that added up to insolence.

She said in a voice like a whiplash, 'Did you come to my mother's party intending to be insulting? Or is it a spur-of-the-moment thing?'

'Insulting?' He sounded genuinely taken aback. Then, unforgivably, he looked amused. Amused and intrigued. 'How have I insulted you?'

Candy was furious. 'Saying I suited you. *Suited* you.'

He chuckled. 'That wasn't quite what I meant.' He came over to her. 'But I'm sorry you consider it an insult, anyway.'

And he bent and kissed her.

Candy's first reaction was outrage. In fact she was so angry that she forgot to be afraid, as she usually was.

She pushed hard at his chest. The forgotten champagne tipped, spilling on to his immaculate jacket. He released her a little, but only to take the champagne flute out of her hand.

'Why don't we put this down?' he said gently. 'You know you're not going to drink it. And it is in the way, wouldn't you agree?'

Candy spluttered. Justin Richmond leaned back a little and put the intrusive glass down on a convenient table. He looked down into her face, those strange eyes dancing.

'And now——'

She tensed. But this was nothing like the brisk brutality her experience had taught her to expect. His mouth just brushed hers, lightly, coolly. His fingertips rested along the rigid line of her spine, without pressure. There was no demand, just a gentle, infinitely courteous savouring of their closeness. All Candy's senses seemed to come alive. With a sigh she felt herself relax against him.

She completely forgot why she had been angry with him. Or even that she had been angry at all.

'Mm. I knew it.' Justin said it softly, not taking his lips from hers.

Her eyes drifted open. She did not remember closing them.

'Knew what?' She hardly recognised her voice.

But his answer was another of those tantalising kisses. Candy locked her arms round his neck and drowned in sensation.

She was vaguely aware that no one she knew would have recognised quiet Candy Neilson in the sensuous woman responding to Justin's lightest touch. She hardly recognised her herself. It was mildly alarming. But there was also satisfaction in leaping the barriers of good behaviour and acquired caution. So this was what it felt like to give in to your impulses, she thought, exhilarated.

At last Justin raised his head. She thought he did it reluctantly, and felt a queer surge of triumph.

'Temptress.' The laughing voice was husky.

He tucked a straying lock of hair back into the sculptured swirls. To the dazed Candy it felt incredibly tender. He held her away from him.

'Where do you want to go?'

'What?' Bewildered, she stared at him.

He touched her mouth with a gentle fingertip.

'We need to talk, I think. But *not* surrounded by your father's neglected Monets. Will you have dinner with me?'

Candy stared harder.

'Dinner? Now? This evening? But what about Mrs Davent?'

'A lower priority. She'll understand.'

'But——'

'Your mother told you to get rid of me,' he reminded her gently. 'How better?'

Candy flushed. He held her face between his hands.

'Trust me.'

So she went with him.

She half expected a discreetly lit fashionable restaurant. But he took her to a smoky cellar. In one corner a band was producing complicated, muffled rhythms while an ebony-skinned man danced a flugelhorn through a range of sounds Candy had never even imagined.

It was crowded, but a cheerful girl directed them to a corner table. She clearly knew Justin. Justin equally clearly knew the menu.

'The burgers are nearly as good as the music,' he said, leaning back in his chair and watching Candy. His eyes were warm. 'But have what you want.'

She looked down at the gingham tablecloth, suddenly confused.

'I—I'm not a connoisseur of burgers.'

It sounded horridly prim. Well-behaved Candy was back again, it seemed. She was furious with herself. But she didn't know how to reverse the crippling self-consciousness.

Justin didn't seem to notice. 'Then this is where you start.' He gave the order. 'And I'll think about wine.'

The waitress nodded. 'I'll come back.'

Candy said impulsively, 'You don't look as if you'd be a connoisseur of burgers either.'

He looked up from the wine list. 'Are you complaining about my age or my attitude?' He sounded amused again.

In spite of her self-consciousness, she smiled.

'Neither. I was thinking more of the three-piece suit.'

He grimaced. 'Jungle camouflage.'

His eyes rested briefly on the emerald and gold choker she wore. It felt as if he had reached out and touched her there at the base of her throat. She put up a hand to the jewel, feeling herself tense.

But he was saying thoughtfully. 'Not unlike your own, I suspect. Maybe even the same jungle.'

Candy was startled. His eyes were steady, a faint question in their depths. The silence between them lengthened until she could hardly bear it. Her eyes fell.

The steady beat of the band beat through her like a pulse, calming her.

She said in her best social manner, 'You think of my mother's cocktail party as a jungle?'

Justin shrugged. 'Maybe not. But you certainly do. I've never seen a girl look so scared. Why on earth go, if you hate the things so much?'

She gasped. The social manner fell away.

'What do you mean?'

'What I say,' he said, bored. 'I don't waste time saying things I don't mean.'

'Is that a health warning?' she challenged.

He gave her another of those unnervingly silent looks. 'If you like,' he said softly at last.

Candy shivered. 'It sounds as if you're trying to intimidate me.'

Justin looked surprised. 'The opposite.'

She thought about that, frowning. 'You mean you want to reassure me?'

The strange eyes glinted. 'That's not the way I'd have put it.'

'Then what?'

'Maybe—invite you to have a little more courage?' he hazarded.

She stared at him. The drums beat. Suddenly she grinned. 'You want to put a bit of backbone into me,' she said at last. 'That's what my granny was always saying.'

Justin's eyebrows flew up. 'A forthright lady.'

'Yes, she was. I miss her.' Candy bit her lip. 'She was my father's mother. She didn't have much patience with either of my parents, I'm afraid. She more or less brought me up, you know.'

'I know nothing about you at all,' Justin said softly. 'Except that you're Leslie Neilson's daughter. And you expect to be eaten alive at parties.'

'It's a reasonable start,' Candy said wryly.

He leaned back in the bentwood chair and looked at her. All around them the diners laughed and the waiters sped in professional breathlessness. There was the clink of glasses, the steady thrum of the band—and the silence between them. It was like a spider's web, intricate, fragile, barely perceptible. And dangerous, thought Candy with a superstitious shiver.

A waiter paused at Justin's shoulder.

'Rioja,' he said, not taking his eyes off Candy.

The waiter made a note and moved off.

'Dance with me,' Justin said.

Candy jumped. The band was producing a complicated syncopated rhythm which the mellow sax made deceptively melting.

'I don't really—er——'

But he was on his feet, his eyes amused.

'Aren't you a connoisseur of dancing either? Stick with me and I'll give you a few hints,' he said with a soft laugh.

Like a mesmerised creature, Candy stood up and put her hand in his. With his fingers loosely linked with her own, he guided her through the indifferent crowd.

The dance-floor was bigger than she had thought. The dancers, too, were a surprise—skinny schoolboys dancing like electric eels, middle-aged black matrons who moved as if they were part of the music, and every age, condition and dress in between. Nobody so much as glanced at them.

Justin took her in his arms. She could smell a faint hint of some woody fragrance as she rested her cheek against his jacket. He moved easily, his whole body turning and responding to the music, taking her with him. To her astonishment, Candy began to feel the tension ebb away. She was even enjoying herself.

He rested his chin on the top of her head. 'Tell me about granny.'

They were swaying lazily in perfect unison.

Candy smiled into his chest. 'She was a Tartar. Hugely independent. She never let my father give her much. She lived in the house she'd been married in till the day she died. She said he used money like Valium—to stop him thinking.' She sighed. 'She always wanted me to get away. She said I feather-bedded my mother.'

Justin's face moved against her hair. Candy's pulse fluttered.

'And do you?' he asked.

She tipped her head back. In the heavy coloured lights of the dance-floor, spirals of smoke were drifting upwards. They looked like the curls from a hundred genie's lamps, Candy thought. She felt light-headed, unlike herself. It was a new sensation—and exhilarating. Her shoulders were moving in rhythm to the infectious beat.

'Perhaps,' she said dreamily.

Justin looked down at her. In the action-painted shadows his expression was oddly grave.

'Does your father treat you the way he treats his paintings?' he asked abruptly.

She shook her head slowly. 'Don't understand.'

His voice was very soft. 'Safe from thieves. Not loved.'

'Oh. Like that.' After a moment, Candy nodded. 'I suppose he does.' She smiled at him brilliantly. 'He thinks a lot about burglars. We have locks and bars all over the house.'

For a moment he held one long, lean hand to the side of her face, holding her whole length against him. They were barely moving their feet but their shoulders swayed in time to the whispery music.

Justin said, 'I don't like locks and bars.'

Candy watched his mouth shape the words. She thought, I wonder if we'll still keep dancing while we kiss? She reached up and touched her lips to his. He was smiling. She could feel it. She thought muzzily, This is wonderful. Why have I never done this before?

And then it hit her like a cold shower—she was in the middle of a dance-floor, twining herself round a man in the way she had seen and been amazed by in other girls at the dances her mother made her go to. A man, moreover, whom her mother had told her was Sir Leslie's implacable rival.

She stopped dead. For a moment the light touch on her spine tightened. Then she was released. Justin looked down at her.

'Suddenly remembered you're hungry?' he asked her, that smile in his voice.

It was an alibi. But Candy was nothing if not honest. 'Backbone ran out,' she said sadly.

For a moment he hesitated. Then he gave a single nod. 'Ah. Well, it was probably time to disentangle anyway.'

It was perfectly friendly, perfectly casual. It could not have been more obvious that it was no big deal for sophisticated Justin Richmond. Candy was grateful for the cavernous lighting as he led the way back to their table. Her expression would have given her away. She was shaken to her depths.

He seated her, and the waiter returned with food and wine. She looked at Justin under her lashes.

What was there about him? The powerful attraction, of course. He was no boy—the experience showed in the handsome, cynical face. But he looked as if he had the controlled strength of an athlete. It was there in the way he danced. Even under the formal city suit it was unmistakable. And he had the most laughing eyes of any man she had ever met. It was all too easy to let down your guard under those warm brown eyes. They seemed to invite you to share the joke that the rest of the world wasn't quick enough to pick up.

He also had the ability to cut the ground from under her with his patient silences. She set her teeth. There was only one way to deal with it. It was not easy, with those thoughtful brown eyes on her, but she, in her turn, preserved silence.

Eventually Justin Richmond drew a sharp breath. The brown eyes narrowed and grew considerably less warm. It was faintly disconcerting, as if he had dropped a mask.

He said almost briskly, 'How old are you?'

Candy almost jumped.

'Twenty-two,' she replied involuntarily.

'Hmm. Why aren't you married?'

Her eyes flared. There were so many reasons, and she wasn't prepared to share any of them with this dangerous, unpredictable man.

'It's not obligatory.'

'True. But it's a way of getting away from the nest. It usually appeals to nicely brought up young ladies like you better than a career, too,' he said dispassionately.

Candy was outraged. Then she gave a little choke of laughter.

'Unfortunately it isn't that easy to fall in love to order. Or I probably would have married by now,' she retorted coolly.

His mouth curled. 'Love isn't essential.'

That flicked her on the raw. She had tried, she had really tried, to keep an open mind when her mother urged... And it was awful. The only man who didn't terrify her was Dave. Whom she loved.

She said sharply, 'Of course it is.'

Justin seemed interested. 'You think so? Why?'

'Well—er——' she floundered, not prepared for this '—without love, it's cheating.'

Justin was amused. 'I don't see why. As long as it was clear and mutually agreed from the start, who would be cheated?'

She shook her head slowly. 'It's—wrong.'

The brown eyes sharpened. '*Moral* objections?' He sounded incredulous.

Candy bit her lip. 'Marriage is...oh, I don't know, maybe it's too important. Too deep to turn into some sort of masquerade.'

He put his elbows on the table and cupped his hands round the glass. The wine looked like blood, she thought.

He looked alert and interested and about as involved as if he were debating the fat stock prices.

'Explain.'

She marshalled her thoughts, and said carefully, 'Marriage doesn't work for a lot of people. I know that it's hell when it goes wrong. But they—most people—go into it in good faith. If we—I—didn't—I'd feel I was letting everyone down. Not necessarily everyone I know. But everyone else who tries to make a marriage work—even if they don't succeed.' She looked at him unhappily. She sounded like a prig again. 'Do you understand?'

There was another, longer pause. Candy's eyes fell. She could feel herself flushing, even while she thought stubbornly, I believe that. I've never said it before, but that's what I really believe. That's why I so hated Tom kissing me and . . .

She looked up. Justin was regarding her with an arrested expression. She shifted uncomfortably. But as soon as their eyes met his face changed, all expression smoothed out of it.

'And you'd think of it as cheating. Yes, I see.' He sounded almost absent. He looked down at his glass. 'It won't be easy . . .'

Candy thought she must have misheard him.

'I'm sorry?'

'Eat your burger,' he said, not attending. 'What about boyfriends?'

'*What*?'

He chuckled. 'Why aren't there any?'

Candy stiffened. 'How do you know there aren't?'

'Because if there were you wouldn't have been standing in that doorway scared to death and all on your own tonight.'

She winced. If only Dave had seen what this man had seen and come with her! Justin reached out across the table and covered her tense, drumming fingers with a warm hand.

'If you were mine,' he said softly, 'you wouldn't have been scared. And you wouldn't have been alone.'

She sat very still. It was like being on the edge of a precipice with no idea of how you got there. She tore her hand away. 'I don't know what you mean.'

He sat back, smiling. 'Yes, you do.'

She stared at him. Although he didn't try to touch her again, she felt as if he was pulling her towards him. It was like Tom all over again: a little wine, a little music, the odd heightened atmosphere that was supposed to make her lose her inhibitions and then...and then... Only that long body would be stronger than Tom's. And, unlike Tom, Justin Richmond wasn't afraid of her complaining to her father. Candy began to shake inside.

Oh, Dave, where are you when I need you?

When she got home Candy went to her own room and called the Centre.

Dave Tresilian answered at once. He stayed in the office, manning it and taking calls from the other services as well as the down-and-outs themselves.

'Homeless Centre. May I help you?'

She felt the tension go out of her.

'Dave? Candy.'

His voice warmed at once. 'Hello, love. How was the party?'

'Grimish. I was detailed to neutralise the enemy. So I had to take him away. We had burgers and danced.'

He laughed. It didn't make her feel any better. He obviously had no interest in the identity of her escort.

'It's a hard life for some.'

'It is,' Candy agreed fervently. 'Dave——'

'Yes?'

But she didn't know what to say to him. Except, Help me—which he thought he was already doing, by taking her on to his voluntary staff. Or, Love me—which was out of the question.

He wished her an affectionate goodnight. Candy carried it to bed with her.

Which meant that it was all the odder that the last thing she remembered before she drifted off into sleep wasn't his voice but Justin Richmond's.

He was saying, 'It won't be easy.'

CHAPTER TWO

CANDY was still turning that enigmatic remark over in her head when she went downstairs the following morning. But what she saw in the kitchen pulled her up short. Justin Richmond flew out of her head as if he had never been there.

The work surfaces were stacked with glasses and plates from last night's party, clean and ready to be put away. Maria was standing in front of the coffee-machine, watching it percolate as if her life depended on it. And in the middle of the kitchen, with empty hands and a queer, blank expression on her face, sat Judith.

She looked up. Candy had the feeling that she was not really seeing her.

Judith said, 'Your father's gone.' She sounded exhausted. 'He was very angry.'

Candy said quietly, 'It's all right, Maria. I'll deal with coffee.'

Looking relieved, Maria went.

'What happened?'

Judith stared at her hands for a moment. 'I've been gambling,' she said at last.

Candy stared at her. '*Gambling*? What...when?'

'In the beginning Molly Stapleton took me. It's a club. You play in the afternoon.' She sounded faintly proud of this surprising knowledge.

'Mrs Stapleton,' said Candy grimly, 'is as rich as Croesus and hasn't anything better to do with her time.'

'Have I?' demanded Judith on a flash of feeling.

Candy stared, shocked.

Her mother caught herself. 'Oh, I'm sorry, darling. I shouldn't have said that. It's just that with you out so much these days—and your father away such a lot—life has seemed a bit empty, somehow. Boring. And roulette was exciting.'

Candy was shaken. She had no idea her mother had been feeling like this. Her inconvenient conscience stirred.

'And now he's found out, has he? Pops?' she asked gently.

'Don't call him that,' Judith said automatically. 'You know he hates it.'

Candy was angry suddenly. 'What's he got to complain about? What else does he do but gamble, with all these companies he buys and sells and hasn't a clue about what they do?'

'He,' said her mother miserably, 'pays for them. I didn't. Or at least, not lately. I ran out of money around Christmas. I knew the cheques would bounce. But I didn't seem able to stop.'

'Oh, my God,' said Candy, realising the full impact that this would have on her father. 'Scandalissimo.'

Judith gave a harsh laugh. 'Absolutely. He got a letter from the bank manager this morning. He said I was no good for anything except wasting money, and he wasn't coming back. And he doesn't even know the worst part yet.'

Candy closed her eyes. 'There's more?' she asked in a carefully neutral voice.

'Yes. The cheques were sent back to the club. They rang me at once, and I said there'd been an oversight. I don't know if they believed me. But one of the people in the office thought it was a good story—you know: NEWSPAPER MAGNATE'S WIFE WRITES DUD CHEQUES. So he took it...'

'No,' said Candy, standing up in horror.

'To Richmond newspapers,' concluded Judith. And began to laugh.

Candy coaxed her mother out of hysterics and then called her doctor. When he came it was plain that he already knew about the gambling debts.

'I gather your father's not here,' he said, writing his prescription at the eighteenth-century desk.

Candy saw no point in pretending. 'Mother thinks he's gone permanently.'

The doctor did not comment. 'She seems to think she's let him down. And you too. Said something about always having been a burden. About you hating her...'

Candy shook her head dumbly.

'Well, someone had better have a word with your father. Preferably,' the doctor added, snapping his case shut, 'someone who isn't afraid of him.'

'I'll do it,' she agreed.

The conversation was terse.

'Your mother told you?' Sir Leslie asked, as soon as Candy announced herself.

'Yes.'

'Stupid woman. I've had enough. She's wasted millions. She can get out of this one on her own.'

'Thank you very much for your support,' Candy murmured.

'Don't take that tone with me,' her father rapped. 'Silly bitch goes from one mess to another. And if you'd spent more time with her it wouldn't have happened. Not a lot to ask, is it? No proper job, won't come into the business. The least you could do is make sure your mother doesn't make an ass of herself. But no, you're off on some mystery tour of your own, only home to eat and sleep. If she gets into bad company and her cheques start to bounce, who's to blame? So don't talk to me about support.'

Candy winced. But she said spiritedly, 'Always got to be someone else's fault, Pops?'

'Maybe she did it deliberately,' he returned.

'Don't be stupid. Of course she didn't. Why should she?'

'Attention-seeking,' said Sir Leslie, shrewdly. 'But, by God, she didn't have to give it to Richmond's paper. It couldn't have happened at a worse time.'

Candy said recklessly, 'What if I persuaded him not to publish?'

There was a fulminating silence at the other end of the telephone.

'Ridiculous. Of course he'll publish. It's just what he needs. He's fighting my bid every step of the way. It's an absolute gift to have a story that my wife can't meet her debts.'

'Then pay them.'

'It's too late for that. And it's about time Judith started taking the consequences of the damned stupid things she does.'

'If I persuade him not to publish, will you pay them?'

The quality of the silence was different this time.

Then Sir Leslie said slowly. 'If you can persuade Justin Richmond to throw away an advantage like that, I'll pay any damned bill you put in front of me.'

'Done,' said Candy.

And put the phone down before either of them could change his or her mind.

The Richmond building was a tall glass arched edifice, more like a giant conservatory than the headquarters of a multi-national company, Candy thought. Alighting from the taxi, she looked up at it. Despite her determination not to be overawed, she could not help contrasting it with the workmanlike brick and steel that

housed her father's offices. It could not have been plainer
that the Richmond family had more taste, more style
and a great deal more money to spend on fixed assets
than Neilson Media. No wonder, Candy thought suddenly, that her father wanted that merger.

She went into the atrium, where fountains played and
a young birch tree grew out of a well. Under it, daffodils
and bluebells waved in the breeze made by the air-
conditioning.

'Very sylvan,' Candy said to the immaculate recep-
tionist. 'I want to see Justin Richmond, please.'

The pleasant expression did not change.

'Have you an appointment?'

'No. My name's Neilson. Candida Neilson.'

The immaculate eyebrows rose just a little. Candy
began to feel nervous. But—to her inner astonishment—
within minutes she was ushered into the executive lift.

Justin Richmond's secretary was a grey-haired woman
of imposing aspect. She was also puzzlingly warm.

'Mr Richmond is on the telephone just at the moment,'
Alison James told her kindly. 'But he knows you're here.'
There was just the faintest hint of amusement in her
voice. 'So nice of you to surprise him.'

Candy bit her lip. 'Er—yes,' she said, bewildered.

'Ah, he's free. Please come this way.'

Candy began to feel like a prisoner for interrogation.
Almost before she was in the door of the big, airy office,
the excuses were tumbling over themselves.

'I didn't mean to interrupt... I mean, I know I should
have rung first, but I didn't think. I'll only be a minute...'

Justin stood up. He looked very tall and slim in his
immaculate dark suit. His dark hair was just slightly disarranged, as if he ran his hands through it while he
worked.

He did not answer her at first. Instead, he looked her
over, a long, cool appraisal which was only just not in-

sulting. It had Candy gritting her teeth and remembering hard that she had come to ask a favour. But she would have liked to scream—preferably while throwing things at him.

'Hello,' he said at last in that husky, amused voice which had lulled her to sleep last night.

His perfect secretary closed the door between their offices very gently.

Justin strolled round the desk and took her jacket. His fingers were cool at the back of her neck, though his touch was quite impersonal. Candy was furious with herself for shivering at that brush of his hand at her nape.

'This is fun,' he told her softly. 'I get so few surprises these days.'

Candy swallowed hard. He was taller than she remembered. Today he was in dark grey, immaculately tailored. It made him look about fourteen times more imposing than Candy had remembered. And what she remembered was bad enough. He towered over her so that she had to look up.

He smiled down at her—that smile that made you feel as if you were under a sun-lamp, Candy thought uneasily. He took her hand. For a wild moment she thought he was going to kiss it, and her whole instinct was to run. But he merely stroked his long fingers over her own, surveying her with a distinctly quizzical air.

'Take all the time you want,' he said. His shoulders shook slightly. 'I'm intrigued.'

Candy tossed back her loosened hair and stepped away from him. She felt more composed with some distance between them. He watched her confusion with appreciation. But he gestured her to a huge black leather sofa, straight-faced.

Reluctantly, Candy sank down. Justin sat on an upright chair and watched her for a moment. She looked away.

Candy could feel her face growing hot. Again she did not know what was happening to her. The glimpse she had had of those steady, world-weary eyes, however, gave her the nasty feeling that Justin knew all too well. She bit her lip and did not know what to say.

'It's charming of you to drop in,' Justin Richmond said at last. 'Why?'

It was almost a relief. At least he was not looking at her in that unnerving silence any more.

Candy looked down at her hands. Her tone was rueful. 'It's not all that easy to explain. I—I realised that in the taxi coming here. I want you to do something—and I don't know what to offer in return.'

Justin's eyebrows flew up. 'You're very frank. So you came here to bargain with me.' He looked at her as if he could see through to the back of her head, she thought. 'Interesting. And your father was on the phone this morning, too, Alison says. Could there be a connection?'

Candy sighed. 'I'm afraid so.'

'Ah,' he said.

There was one of the now familiar silences as Candy tried and failed to find a way of broaching the subject.

'It's my mother,' she blurted at last.

Justin made a small movement as if she had astonished him, but was immediately still again.

'One of your——' she sought for an appropriate word—scandal sheets wouldn't do, nor would filthy rags '—papers has got a story about her. My—my father is...' She found she could not go on.

His eyes narrowed. He looked at her, but she thought he did not really see her. The clever brain was at work, sifting and discarding until he came to the truth.

'I can imagine,' Justin said eventually. 'So you want me to lean on the editor?'

Candy flushed. 'It sounds bad, put like that.'

Justin stood up and walked away from her. He stood looking down into the courtyard twenty storeys below. When he spoke his voice was hard.

'It is bad,' he assured her. 'Unlike your father, I believe in editorial independence.'

So did Candy in theory. She hesitated, torn. He saw it.

'Why don't you try telling me the lot?' Justin Richmond invited softly.

And, to her surprise, she did. She told him everything, including her father's infidelities, her mother's debts—even her own contribution with her recent absences. When she had finished, he was silent.

'Scandal—that sort of scandal—would finish her. Especially now. And she's sure Pops will leave her.'

His eyes were shrewd. 'You don't agree?'

Candy shook her head. 'He's been on the brink of it for years, if you believe him.'

She tried to sound cool, but her voice broke. The brown eyes narrowed. For a moment she felt as if he could see the tears, the fights, with Candy carrying messages and desperately trying to placate both sides; it was as if she were a film he could run forward or backward at will.

She shook herself. No one was that perceptive. Especially not someone you had only just met.

'I don't know, and I don't suppose he does. I don't care any more.' She realised with a little shock how cold and hard she sounded.

Justin heard it too. He put his head on one side, his eyes bright with interest. 'You're very cynical for one so young.'

'The child is the father of the man. Or, in this case, woman,' Candy replied, not meeting his eyes.

'Or, in this case, schoolgirl,' he corrected gently.

She lifted her eyes at that, indignant. 'I'm not. I'm twenty-two. I told you last night.'

His eyes flickered. At once she wondered if she was not supposed to mention last night. Perhaps he thought of it as some sort of shameful aberration that he was already regretting.

'I mean——'

But he interrupted. 'No one,' he said calmly, 'would believe it.'

There was no sign of shame or any other emotion there. Candy saw it with mixed feelings. Had last night meant so little, then? In the sophisticated round of his days, she had to suppose it was probably nothing very memorable. She prepared to be very, very cool.

'I'm not a child. I know the way the world works,' she said. 'With parents like mine, it'd be hard not to.'

'A bit of the world, maybe,' he allowed. He sat back in his chair, playing with his fountain-pen, watching her. 'The bit that buys and deals and bargains. You were going to offer me a bargain, weren't you?'

'Er—yes.'

She pushed her hands through her hair, embarrassed. She could feel the warmth in her cheeks, and was perfectly certain that he had noticed.

'What were you going to offer?' he asked softly. 'Your influence with your father to make him withdraw his offer for my company? Your shares in Neilson Media, so I could make a counter-bid?'

Her father would be furious. Candy swallowed.

'Is that what you want?'

His eyes were very steady. 'No, I don't think it is.'

She gave a long sigh. 'And you must have more than enough money already, so *that's* no good.'

'More than enough,' he agreed, amused.

'You wouldn't settle for my undying gratitude, I suppose?' she said, trying for a lightness she did not feel.

His eyes rested on her thoughtfully.

'That would rather depend on how it was expressed.'

There was a long, screaming silence in which Candy felt as if she were being slowly stretched until she snapped.

She said huskily, 'I don't believe you said that.'

He leaned back in the chair, laughing. 'Believe it.'

She sprang to her feet, suddenly gloriously angry.

'It's crazy. It's medieval. You're not some ancient movie mogul with a casting couch, for heaven's sake.'

Justin seemed even more amused. 'I was thinking,' he explained gently, 'of marriage.'

Candy felt her jaw drop.

'What do you think of the idea?' he asked, with a gleam in his eye that was pure mockery.

Candy swallowed hard, and said with as much coolness as she could muster in the circumstances, 'Ridiculous.'

Justin grinned. '*Not* polite,' he murmured.

She ignored that.

'You don't want to marry,' she said.

The smile grew. 'Who told you that?' And before she could answer, 'Anyway, nor do you. It would give us something in common.'

She groaned. 'This is no time to be making bad jokes.' You're old enough . . . that is, you're quite old enough to be married already if you wanted to be.'

'No, I am not old enough to be your father,' he said calmly, diagnosing what she had been going to say. 'And I have been married. Marianne and I divorced several years ago, and I've never felt that the experiment bore repeating. Until now.'

He didn't say he could get all the female companionship he needed without offering marriage. It was written all over him.

Candy asked, 'So why change now?'

Justin took so long to answer that she thought he was not going to. When he did, he seemed to have stopped laughing.

'Because this bid is turning into a serious pain. I want your father and his minions off my back. If we had a co-operation agreement—cemented by a dynastic marriage—it could stave off a full merger. And I could go back to running the business without my shareholders ringing me up every ten seconds.'

Candy stared. 'And for that you'd sacrifice your freedom? Is that enough?'

There was a little pause.

'You're shrewder than you look,' Justin said. He did not sound entirely pleased. 'No, of course it's not enough.'

A pulse began to beat violently at the base of her throat. Candy felt as if she would choke. But she forced herself to ask calmly, 'Then what?'

Justin hesitated. The lids dropped over the deep-set eyes so that he looked like a judge—or an emperor deciding on a whim whether a slave would live or die, thought Candy. She shivered. She was not usually so fanciful.

Justin said, 'When we talked—I was impressed.' He looked at her straight. 'You take marriage seriously. I like that.'

'But we don't know each other.' It was almost a wail.

He nodded. 'It would be a gamble, of course.'

There was another longer pause.

Then he said, amazingly, 'I like that too. I've always been a gambler.'

Candy's pulse was slamming so hard that she felt it would shake her apart. She gritted her teeth.

'You mean the whole works? Sex and children and everything?'

His teeth gleamed in a tiger's smile. He was laughing at her.

'The *Book of Common Prayer* puts it more gracefully, but that's about the size of it,' he agreed. 'It should be fun.'

'*Fun*!'

'Oh, yes, I think so. Don't you?'

The look he gave her was calculated to bring any woman to her knees, Candy saw. The fact that all it did for her was make her shake with fright seemed unfair. The brown eyes with their hint of laughter drifted down the primrose shirt and up again to where the pulse was beating so frantically.

Instinctively Candy put up both hands and drew the points of the starched collar together. It was a revealing little gesture, and she knew it too late. Without it, there was just a chance that he might not have noticed her agitation. Although she didn't think there was really much that he had missed in their discussion.

She said in a voice that croaked, 'I—don't know.'

'No,' he agreed. 'No, I can see that. Would it help if I said we could take things slowly? At your own pace?'

Candy was shaken. 'I never meant to marry. I've always——' She broke off.

Justin nodded. 'Very understandable, given your role models. But you're really too young to take a negative decision like that.' He smiled at her almost tenderly. 'You're only scared, you know. And we can do something about that.'

'You sound almost as if you *want* to marry me,' Candy said slowly.

Justin was enigmatic. 'But I do. Haven't I just proposed to you?'

'Yes, but...'

She could feel the force of his will-power like a tangible thing, as if he had reached out and looped a hawser round her. She felt almost physically dragged towards him—and those warm, laughing eyes were fiercely determined.

Candy did not understand it. She looked away, not wanting to understand it. She felt threatened. On the brink. Terrified.

There was only one thing to do in an extremity: tell the truth. No one believed you, Candy reminded herself.

'You're right,' she said. She drew a long breath, and did the only thing she could. 'I don't know why, but the very idea terrifies me. I must be more juvenile than I thought.'

He didn't say anything at all. Candy held her breath. Then, meeting his eyes, she realised that her tactic had failed. Because Justin Richmond *did* believe her. Her last defence was gone.

'Damn,' she said, feeling rather foolish.

She waited for him to protest, persuade, maybe to taunt her. But he did nothing. For a moment of pure embarrassment she wondered whether he would reply at all.

But eventually he drew a long breath. Then he said, 'We'll talk about it later.'

'Later? But...'

He gave her a sweet smile. 'I still have to find out what my editors have on your mum's indiscretions. And, although I don't dictate what they print, I can sometimes ask a pointed question or two. Like how much libel damages we're risking.'

Candy's eyes widened. He laughed and, leaning forward, kissed her very lightly on the lips.

She went rigid. It was a casual contact, barely a caress, but it spoke of possession. He had made her feel like that before. Without appearing to notice it. Did he make every woman he touched feel like that too?

'I'll see where we stand. And I'll call you later,' he told her lightly. 'Think about it, though, will you?'

CHAPTER THREE

CANDY could never afterwards remember clearly what she did after she left the Richmond building. She thought she walked. She remembered cold streets and a flurry of wind when she turned corners. But she did not register anything until she arrived at the Homeless Centre.

All she could think of was the cool voice with its occasional flashes of treacherous warmth; of the level gaze; of the humour that seemed occasionally to be at something she could not see. And of that last casual kiss that had set some sort of seal on their unagreed bargain.

She must have looked like a ghost. Helen looked up from her typewriter when Candy walked in, and sprang immediately to her feet.

'You're frozen. Coffee,' she stated, the moment her hand touched Candy's. 'What's been happening to you?'

Candy shook her head dazedly. 'I'm not sure.'

Justin had happened. Candy shivered. She did not understand him. She sensed that he wanted her in some obscure way that left her half flattered, half afraid. But she did not really know what had happened to her in that interview. Except that she felt as if it had swept all the hard-won rock from under her feet and flung her back in the quicksand of emotion and demand.

She accepted the steaming mug.

'I—I'm sorry. I'm not making much sense. Even to myself.'

Helen hesitated. 'Want to talk about it?'

Candy shut her eyes. 'I'm not sure I can.'

What would it be like? What could it possibly be like? She had never in her remotest dreams imagined herself going to bed with someone like Justin. Even Dave—well, she had had her fantasies, of course, but mostly they consisted of his rescuing her from dire peril or—occasionally—the reverse. She had never allowed her imagination to touch on anything physical. Whereas, after Justin's laughing proposal, she could not banish it.

Helen said worriedly, 'You look pole-axed. Having problems with the parents?'

Helen knew that Candy wanted to work at the Centre full time—that she was waiting for the right moment to tell her family. Candy, with the reticence of a lifetime, had not said there would be difficulties. But Helen must have deduced it.

She said wryly. 'Not in the way you mean.'

Helen offered again, 'If you want to talk——'

But almost the only belief that Judith had in common with her husband was that you didn't discuss family. 'Don't wash dirty linen in public,' Gran Neilson used to say. And Candy had got used to keeping her own counsel.

She had not told anyone about the fights, the enmity, the accusations, the reproaches. And now she could not tell kind, concerned Helen what was wrong. She had never had a real friend because she had never been able to tell anyone else what her real life was like—except, she realised with a little start, Justin Richmond last night. What had *happened* to her last night?

She shook her head. 'I haven't the habit. But thanks, Helen.'

'Maybe you should talk to Dave,' Helen said doubtfully.

Candy shook her head again, more vigorously. If Dave Tresilian had come with her to that party as she had asked, she thought with a glimmer of indignation, none of this would have happened. Except Judith's gambling would have happened. Except Sir Leslie's threats would have happened. Only, if she and Justin had not met, he would not have offered her this frightening bargain as a solution.

Why did it have to be marriage? It had turned her father into a tyrant and her mother into a cringing slave. Candy didn't want to be any man's slave.

'No,' she said, 'not Dave. Look, Helen, I'm really not feeling great. Could you...?'

'You go home and lie down,' Helen told her. 'I'll organise cover. Don't worry about it. You look like death.'

'Thank you,' said Candy drily.

She went back to the Mayfair mansion, but not to lie down. She hesitated for a moment, then went to her mother's room.

Judith was fidgeting round her boudoir, hollow-eyed and grey under the make-up. Sir Leslie had not rung.

'Darling, will you ring your father for me? Tell him...'

Candy couldn't bear the anxious expression, the pleading. She had done it all too many times before. She looked down at Judith's desk, littered with unopened letters, witness to her empty, anxious morning.

'Mother, why is it so bad if he goes? He's not exactly an ideal husband.'

Judith said hopelessly, 'You don't understand.'

'No, I don't,' Candy agreed. 'He's rude and demanding and he has a foul temper. And you're afraid of him,' she added shrewdly. 'What's worth hanging on to?'

Judith stared. 'He's my husband. My life.'

'Then maybe you ought to find something better to do with your life.'

But it was hopeless. Judith became hysterical at the very thought of Leslie Neilson leaving for good.

In the end Candy left her, her own dilemma unconfided and unresolved.

If only someone would listen to *me*, she thought. I can't run a courier service between my parents for the rest of my life. But what am I going to do? And then, sneaking in under cover came the thought, if only Justin Richmond weren't who he is, I could ask *him*.

In the end she compromised, giving Dave Tresilian a carefully edited story later that evening. They were alone with the telephones while the other helpers took the vans of hot food and drink round the streets. For once, the phones were silent.

Candy perched on the corner of Dave's desk and told her tale. Or most of it. She did not tell him about Justin. For some reason that she was not quite sure about herself, she suspected that Dave's famous sympathy might run out if she described Justin's proposal.

'What do you think I ought to do?'

Dave tilted his chair back, pushing his fingers through his red-gold hair. He was a tall, impressive man with the physique of a prize fighter and the eyes of an evangelist. Or so Candy thought. His presence in a room somehow made it smaller.

He listened carefully, stroking his ginger beard.

'Your mother's taking it badly?'

Candy sighed. 'She seems to think it's terminal. Why she isn't glad to be out of it, I don't know.'

Dave gave her a faintly exasperated look. 'Your father's a very rich man.'

Candy stared at him. He looked away after a minute.

He said at last, roughly, 'Look it's all very well to pretend that money doesn't matter when you've got plenty. If you don't know where the next meal is coming from—or where you'll sleep tonight—it's different.'

Candy felt stunned. She said slowly, 'We're not talking about my mother, are we, Dave?'

He flushed an unbecoming tomato colour.

'I thought—I was hoping—that is, I didn't see why your father shouldn't contribute. You were interested and you were his only child. And we *need* that new hostel,' he added not very lucidly.

'My *father* . . . ?'

She had not realised that Dave even knew who her father was. She had told them her name when she first went to the Homeless Centre, and they had her phone number for emergencies, but she had never talked about her parents. She never did.

'Ah.' She stood up. 'I see.'

Dave stood up too. He seemed puzzled. But Candy noticed that he would not meet her eyes.

It was true. They did need the hostel. She had spent days in the Centre addressing mailshots to possible donors. It had not occurred to her that Dave had his eye on her father, though.

'Was that why you let me come and help?' Candy asked quietly. 'Why you always had *time* for me?'

He looked indignant. 'Of course not. I didn't even know you were that Candida Neilson to begin with. You were hard-working and obviously committed. It was later . . .'

'It was later that you promoted me to confidante and organiser,' Candy said steadily. 'When you realised.'

Her throat was beginning to burn. Some of it was rage, of course, but some was straightforward grief. How could he? She had thought he'd recognised her determination and promoted her because of it. And all the time it was because he knew she was a rich girl whose father might be induced to fund the next project. He could not have told her more clearly that she did not matter—either as a colleague or as a woman.

At the thought of her romantic dreams of this man, Candy's whole body flinched. Well, at least he did not know. At least he had never guessed that she was in love with him. She almost hated him for a second or two for that blindness.

Dave was saying, 'Look, you can do us a lot of good, Candy. The Centre isn't glamorous, though it's desperately needed. Someone with your background actually helping—well, it's a gift. If you could talk your father into putting up some money we'd be in a whole new ball game.'

'Yes,' said Candy in a cool, precise little voice. She felt as if she were bleeding to death. 'Yes, I see what you mean. And if I married Justin Richmond I could ask for a brand new hostel as a wedding present, couldn't I?'

Even in his absorption, he noticed that.

'Marry Justin Richmond? But I thought he and your father were at daggers drawn!' he exclaimed.

There was a nasty silence while she looked at him.

'How very much more you know about my family than I realised, Dave,' Candy said, marvelling.

He looked flustered. 'It's been in all the papers. Everyone said your father was trying to unseat the top guy at Richmonds and take the group over. That's Richmond, isn't it?'

'That's him,' confirmed Candy grimly.

Dave drew a long breath. 'And he wants to marry you?' He sounded awed. 'That's wonderful. We need a higher profile chair——' He caught sight of her face and stopped dead. He gave her a weak smile. 'Of course you mustn't marry anyone you don't want to, love.'

Candy drew a long breath. That careless, meaningless endearment was the last straw. She had been building a lot of dreams on those 'loves' and 'honeys' of Dave Tresilian. She was suddenly savage.

'Thank you,' she said coolly. 'Disinterested advice is so hard to come by.'

He winced. But Candy was already gathering her things. She ignored him.

Candy went home in a cold rage such as she could not remember experiencing before. It was nearly two when she got in. Her mother had gone to bed. There was a plaintive note on the hall table. Candy glanced at it cursorily and then screwed it up. She looked at her watch.

It was a crazy hour to telephone anyone. Impetuously she picked up the telephone. Justin answered on the fourth ring. She was surprised. So he wasn't in bed either. Or he had a phone by the bed. Though he didn't sound sleepy.

'Candy,' she said curtly.

'Ah.' His voice warmed. 'Solved it?'

'I'll marry you.'

She could feel his startled withdrawal down the wire.

'You,' she reminded him harshly, 'suggested it.'

'So I did,' he said slowly. 'But I didn't expect...'

So he hadn't thought she'd agree. Perhaps he didn't even want her to agree. Two rejections in one evening, Candy. Well done. Just as well you don't think you're irresistible, she told herself fiercely.

'Second thoughts?' she mocked, transferring her anger and humiliation into sarcasm.

Justin gave a soft laugh. 'Lots. And third and fourth thoughts. And all—interesting. I take it you've been thinking along the same lines yourself?'

Candy ignored the gentle teasing. She noted the sensual suggestion in his voice and it infuriated her. He wasn't baiting the trap with spurious affection, like Dave. But no doubt he was quite as clear as Dave had been about what he wanted from malleable Candy Neilson.

She damned all men and their nasty, conniving minds. Under her breath. She said coolly, 'I've taken advice. It's unanimous. I'll marry you.' And, when there was silence, added in a sharp tone, 'I'm convinced.'

Justin was thoughtful. 'That's a pity. I'd hoped to convince you myself.'

It surprised her. How had she allowed herself to forget his talent for wrong-footing her? Candy shivered. There was a blatant promise in the husky voice that, in her present frame of mind, felt more like a threat.

To hide the sensation—as much from herself as from him—she said in a crisp voice, 'We'll need to talk, of course. When and where?'

There was a pause. She could feel that sharp brain working, calculating. There was something here he did not understand, and he did not like it.

At last he said smoothly, 'Yes, I think you *do* need to talk. Why don't you come over here? I'm happier on my home territory.'

'Fine.' I don't believe I'm doing this, Candy thought. I must have taken leave of my senses. 'When?'

'Why not now?'

'*Now*?' Her mouth went instantly dry. 'You must be out of your mind. It's too late.'

'It wasn't too late to phone,' he reminded her. 'And I'm not sleepy. Are you?'

Candy swallowed. She had, she supposed, asked for this. She had not expected to have her hand called so soon, but she had known it must happen. Cold shivers were running up and down her spine. She would have to stop that before she saw him.

She replied slowly, 'I suppose not.'

'Good girl,' he said surprisingly. 'Where are you? I'll come and get you.'

'No!' It was a fierce reaction, surprising her. 'No,' she said more calmly. 'I've got my car. Give me the address.'

He did so and she put the phone down.

Rather to her surprise, Justin's home turned out to be in a side-street in Kensington. She had expected something grander and more private. The last place that would have occurred to her was a simple door at the side of a block of high-street shops. It was, she thought wryly, hardly his image, living above the shop.

She told him so, a little breathlessly, when he answered the bell. Justin looked amused.

'Hardly my shop,' he pointed out gently. 'Can I take your coat?'

Reluctantly, Candy surrendered her thigh-length denim jacket. It was no great protection against the cold, but as he hung it up in the cupboard she began to shiver again. She had had bouts of that convulsive shivering all the way here in the car. He noticed it, frowning.

'You're cold. Come upstairs. I'll get the fire going.'

She followed him up pale carpeted stairs. When she got to the top she stopped in amazement.

'Oh,' she said, looking round.

It was a long room, running the length of the parade of shops below, she judged. For the moment the windows were hidden by great swaths of apricot brocade that fell from ceiling to floor, but clearly the place would be full of light during the day. The opposite wall, however, was the really startling thing. It was entirely covered by a stylised tiger picked out against a spare brushed landscape of bamboo and thin trees. And it was gold.

'I told you I didn't put my works of art in prison and forget about them,' Justin reminded her softly.

She gave him a sharp look. He met it blandly. He crossed the polished wooden floor to the grate at the far end of the room. He bent, and she heard a match strike, a whoosh, and there was a flickering fire.

'Phoney,' Justin said cheerfully, 'but warm. Come and toast your toes.'

She walked the length of the room very carefully. There was not much in it—a couple of large green and black urns, an eight-foot palm in a stone trough, a Chinese silk rug—but she suspected everything was unique.

Candy perched on the edge of the large cane chair he indicated. Justin dropped carelessly on to another rug in front of the flames. He looked alert and interested.

'I think you'd better explain.'

Candy frowned. 'Explain what? You proposed. I agreed. Who needs a post-mortem?'

He gave a soft laugh. 'This morning, as I recall, you were saying that you thought you'd never marry.'

'That was before you offered me your bargain.'

He leaned back and looked at her, a small smile curling his mouth. 'And you haven't even asked whether I'm going to keep my side of it,' he pointed out gently. 'So tell me.'

Candy swallowed. 'Tell you what?'

He made a large gesture. 'Everything. Why you're a rich girl who's scared of parties, a young girl who doesn't know a good burger when she tastes it, a bright girl who sits at home and sews a fine seam. And why I'm your way out.'

Candy stared at him. The impulse that had got her here was beginning to waver. She looked at the clever, kind, unreadable face and her resolve disappeared. She felt tears well up.

Justin leaned forward and pressed a switch. The wall lights and the table lamp went out. They were left with just the flickering light of the fire.

The tears, released, began to tumble down her shadowed cheeks. Candy found a crisp white square pressed into her hands. It was Justin's handkerchief. She pressed her face into it. A smell of woodland rose faintly to her nostrils.

He did not try to touch her. He moved back, saying nothing.

When the paroxysm was over, Candy blew her nose.

'Thank you,' she said.

He did not answer directly. Instead he told her, 'You really had better tell me what's going on.'

She bit her lip. He looked so self-contained. Now that her eyes had accustomed themselves to the shadows, she could see that the dark hair was a little disarranged, his eyes bright with amusement. The long-fingered hands were very beautiful, she noticed with a slight shock, beautiful and restless.

She pushed a hand through her tumbled hair.

'You must think I'm being a real pain. I don't know what came over me.'

'Then it was probably long overdue,' Justin said tranquilly. 'As for what I think of you—I'll pass, just for the moment. But what brought on the storm?'

Candy sighed deeply. 'It's been a fraught thirty-six hours.'

'And how much of that was my fault?'

'A good question.' She blew her nose again.

'So answer it.'

She shifted uncomfortably. 'I—I'm not sure. In one way none of it was your fault. In another—it's all down to you.' The words sounded like an accusation. She said hurriedly, 'I'm sorry. I didn't mean——'

'Oh, but I think you did.' He sounded quite unoffended. He looked at her frowningly. 'Candida, tell me—what would you have done, if I hadn't asked you to marry me?'

'Done?'

He made an impatient gesture. 'Now. Because you've been brewing up for some sort of crisis, haven't you?'

She almost gasped. 'How did you know that?'

'My dear girl, you were simmering with it last night. It was evident. You were like a flame about to go up.'

She was surprised and not entirely pleased.

'You're very observant.'

'And very discriminating,' Justin murmured. There was a smile in his voice.

Candy didn't understand him. But she was not going to say so. She was beginning to realise how little she knew about him.

'Well, I didn't feel like a flame,' she said ruefully. 'I was trying to nerve myself to tell my parents——'

He sat up straighter. 'Yes? Flying the nest at last?'

She gave a choke of laughter at the unexpectedly tart question. 'You sound like Gran Neilson. That's the sort of thing she was always saying. Well, telling me to do, really.'

'She sounds excellent,' said Justin drily. 'But why did you have to nerve yourself? They couldn't have expected you to stay home forever. What did you want to do? Hit the Samarkand trail with the wrong guy?'

Candy gave another watery chuckle. She was beginning to feel better under this bracing approach.

'No, I'm not much of an adventurer, I'm afraid.'

'Not even with boyfriends?'

The question hung in the air for too long. Candy swallowed hard. '*Particularly* not with boyfriends,' she said in a low voice.

'Ah.'

He moved. She tensed. But he was only stretching lazily in the firelight.

'So what were you going to do?'

'I was going to work full time at the Homeless Centre,' she told him simply.

'Good God.' His tone was blank.

'I've been going there on a voluntary basis for some time. I—when Gran died, I wanted to do something— you know, to make people's lives better. There's so much pain,' she said, trying to explain. 'When she was ill, I couldn't because I spent most of my time with her. Pops gave her nurses but he never went there, and she was lonely. Afterwards, one of the nurses I got to know suggested I go and help out with her one night. I've been doing it ever since.'

'And you wanted to turn it into a profession,' Justin said thoughtfully.

She flushed, unseen. 'It sounds stupid put like that.'

'Why do you say that?' he asked sharply. 'Of course it doesn't sound stupid. Is that what they said? Your parents?'

Candy shook her head. 'I haven't—that is, Mother told me about this gambling thing and Pops said it wouldn't have happened if I hadn't been out so much and—and——'

He picked up the handkerchief from the carpet at her feet and handed it to her.

'I begin to see,' he said thoughtfully. 'Even so—there must have been men in your life before. Why haven't you cast any of them as Galahad?'

Candy sat upright. 'What do you mean?'

'You need a rescuer,' Justin said. 'Or you think you do. Why haven't you found one?'

She thought about Tom, and shivered.

She said with difficulty, 'I'm not very—responsive. I—should have told you that before.'

Her head fell. She waited, fingers clenched round the damp rag that was his exquisitely laundered handkerchief. There was a draining silence.

But all he said, when he finally spoke, was, 'Are you sure?'

Candy's head came up.

'Response,' he explained gently, 'depends on circumstances. And—er—people. Don't you think?'

In the flickering shadows Justin looked remote. She remembered suddenly that he was the man her father most feared—a cool, powerful businessman and a considerable strategist. He was watching her. But there was no hint of what was passing through that clever brain. She swallowed.

Very slowly, he put out his hand and picked up a strand of her tangled hair. He held it out so that the firelight played along its length, striking gold and red and even green lights from it.

'Beautiful', he said in a thoughtful voice. 'Yes, there must have been plenty of volunteers for Galahad.'

Candy said hurriedly, staring into the fire, 'There was one. His people are friends of my parents. He—made it very obvious that he wanted to marry the daughter of a rich man.'

In the shadows his eyes were shrewd. 'Not much of a candidate for Galahad,' Justin observed smoothly. 'Was he the one you didn't respond to?'

Remembering her shock at Tom's cheerful manhandling, Candy winced.

'You could put it like that.'

'What happened?' he asked gently.

But she flinched from the question, turning her head so that the long hair swirled. It hid her expression.

Justin waited. At last he sighed. 'Look, my dear——'

Candy spun round in her chair, facing him in the shadows. Her voice was high and breathless.

'Don't patronise me,' she said fiercely. 'You asked me to marry you, remember. It wasn't my idea. You just sprang it on me. And I didn't ask you for any explanations, did I?'

'That's not quite the way I remember it,' Justin said evenly.

But Candy swept on, scarcely hearing.

'Oh, no. I came to ask a perfectly reasonable favour. And what did you do? Offer me some crazy bargain. Did I start to pick you over like—like—like a tray of bargain remnants?'

'Candida——'

'No, I didn't. I went away and thought about it seriously. Because I thought you *meant* it seriously.'

She flung up her head. The electric tumble of curls danced in the firelight like a halo. She was quite unaware of it.

'You made me believe you meant it,' she said fiercely. 'Didn't you?'

'Listen——'

'*Didn't* you?'

Justin said something harsh under his breath. He was looking at her almost angrily, she thought. But his voice was perfectly level when he said, 'Yes, I meant it.'

'Well, then——'

'It's not quite as simple as that.'

'Why isn't it?'

Justin looked down at his hands and flexed the long fingers. He appeared to be choosing his words with care.

'You've had a bad time. All those warring parties. I can see that. But—has it not occurred to you that there are bound to be—other fights?'

Candy was suspicious. 'Who with?'

A small smile curled his mouth. It was not a particularly pleasant smile.

'Let us say, for the sake of argument, with me,' he said evenly.

The fight drained out of Candy. She looked at him in amazement. The loose-limbed figure was deceptively relaxed but, even sprawled on the rug as he was, there was no diguising the strength of the jaw or the clever, intent gaze. He looked like a man no one would want as an enemy. She was shaken by a spurt of laughter.

'No way.' She shook her head. 'Absolutely not. You're out of my league. I wouldn't take you on.'

Justin flashed her a look that, just for an instant and even in the friendly shadows, made her gasp. At once he was cool again, with that composed expression on the handsome face, but Candy felt as if lightning had struck right beside her.

Justin said smoothly. 'What if I started it? What are you going to do then?'

Candy was still shaken. 'You won't have any reason to.' She was fervent. 'No provocation at all, I swear.'

He said with sudden weariness, 'Everything you do is a provocation.'

And reached for her.

Candy was tired. She had not expected Justin to touch her, and she was not fast enough to evade that swift strike. In the blink of an eye he had uncoiled himself from the rug so that he was on one knee beside her chair. With one small, strong movement he had her by the shoulders, hard against his chest.

Candy's head went back. Her eyes unfocused.

Justin said, 'For instance, what are you going to do now?'

He sounded amused but there was something else there as well, she thought dimly, something angry. Why was he angry with her, if she had agreed to do what he wanted? In the body that loured over her there was angry tension in every muscle.

She was too tired, she realised suddenly. Too tired for more scenes, more emotion. Too tired to stand up to that overwhelming force she sensed in Justin. She closed her eyes.

'What do you want me to do?' she heard herself say in a whisper.

He froze. For a second Candy thought she had shocked him. Then he gave a soft laugh. It was, she thought, trembling, the iciest sound she had ever heard.

'If that's the way you want to play...' he murmured.

The cool, strong hands moved on her, disposing her more conveniently against him. She had never, thought

Candy, shaken, felt so much like a *thing* in her life. She tried to struggle away, but it was too late. He had her in a grip of iron in the exact position in which she was most helpless.

Justin looked down at her. The dark face was mocking.

'Let me show you, darling.'

CHAPTER FOUR

WOULD it have been any better if she had been more experienced? Later Candy wondered. Until that explicit caress she had not even considered the possibility that Justin might desire her. As it was, she froze.

It was not at all like Tom's proprietorial briskness. It was not like anything she had ever known. His mouth on her skin seemed to spin a web of shadows round her. Although he could not have been gentler, it was terrifying. All Candy's instincts for self-protection sprang to life.

One moment Justin was kissing her; the next she had torn herself away, white-faced and incoherent.

'Don't. Oh, please, stop.' Her voice was shaking so much, she hardly recognised it.

At first she thought Justin was going to take no notice. There was a strange intent glitter in his eyes. The dark, handsome face looked almost savage. But then he seemed to gather all his strength together, and stepped away from her.

Candy collapsed in a huddle against the cane chair. Her hand went to her cheek. Justin watched her, the glitter dying out of his eyes. Eventually he moved. She flinched; but he was only sitting down in the chair opposite.

He said, 'Stop shaking.'

Hardly knowing what she did, Candy shook her head. Under his impatient fingers, her hair had tangled irretrievably. The auburn strands trailed across her cheek, her mouth. She put up a hand to push them away.

Justin closed his eyes briefly.

Her voice coming back under her command, Candy said, 'I don't want...'

The brown eyes flew open. They were rueful.

'Evidently. At least...' He hesitated. His face looked more like an emperor's than ever, she thought, remote and austere. He said carefully, 'Forgive me, but it seems to me you don't know what you want from one minute to the next.'

Candy sat up. She managed to meet his eyes. He was pale, she saw; the dark eyes were almost black and the thin, handsome mouth set in a hard line. He looked angry.

She lifted her chin and hissed, 'You didn't give me much of a chance to *say*.'

His mouth twisted. 'What do you expect, for heaven's sake? A formal debate with votes taken?'

Candy stiffened. 'I expect the right to say no.'

Justin passed a weary hand over his face. The dark hair flopped forward. Even feeling as she did, Candy had to suppress the instinct to brush it back.

'Of course,' he said quietly.

Candy's colour rose in a wave. She shook her head so that her hair fell forward, but it was not much of a disguise. She knew that, in the surprisingly strong embrace, she had lost her head completely.

'I'm sorry if I gave you the wrong impression,' she said stiffly.

She had never imagined losing her head like that; she had not known it was possible. It was a revelation—and not a welcome one.

Justin had stripped away a comfortable curtain she was not even aware of. And behind the curtain was revealed a quivering creature with a whole range of animal appetites Candy had never suspected. She could not have been more shocked if she had found herself wanting to kill someone. She bent her head and did not answer.

Justin gave a sharp sigh. 'I must be losing my touch,' he said at last wryly. 'Don't worry, little one. I was at fault. I read the signs wrong.'

Candy winced. It sounded as if he was mildly annoyed with himself, not as if it mattered to him. He gave no sign of realising the inner turmoil she was in. Her tongue felt locked.

There was a long and painful silence while he looked at her. Candy bit her lip and concentrated on the fire. It was not difficult to tell that his thoughts would not be complimentary.

'You said you didn't want a cheating marriage,' he mused.

Candy shuddered. 'I know. I didn't *realise...*'

Justin drew a sharp little breath. But all he said was, 'And now you do?'

Candy raised her head. He met her swimming eyes. His mouth was rueful. But his eyes were unreadable. She saw, though, that at least he did not seem particularly angry any more—not as he had a moment ago. In a way it was a relief.

But it left her even more anxious, in another way. At least she knew where she was with anger, even if she did not understand it.

She said, 'I don't understand...'

Justin leaned forward and looked at her gravely. It was not easy, but she met his look. She felt as if she had nothing left to hide.

'You always have a right to say no,' he told her at last. He hesitated. 'You always will. Only—are you sure that marriage is what you want, Candida?'

She felt a flicker of indignation. 'But you said——'

'I said a lot of things,' he cut in drily. 'But not that I was a saint. Or a celibate.'

She flushed.

'Think about it a little,' Justin advised. 'There are worse things than a family row or two. I've told you what I want. But I'm old enough to have discovered it from experience. As you pointed out this morning. But you're...' He paused, then said evenly, 'Young. And quite lovely. You must have had some dreams. Has no one made you want to turn them into fact?'

She shivered. There had never been anyone who made her feel as if she had walked into a furnace-blast at the touch of his mouth.

She shook her head.

'No dreams at all?' Justin sounded fascinated and slightly appalled.

'Not about——'

'Oh, my God,' he said in a resigned tone.

The fiery head drooped. 'I'm not much of a bet, am I?' she muttered.

He gave an odd little laugh. 'That's the sort gamblers like. Long odds, amazing rewards.' He sounded amused again, cool and rueful and in control. 'Though these are longer than I bargained for.' He chuckled. 'You were offering nil provocation, if I recall? Well, stick to that and we'll be all right.'

Candy bit her lip. Justin sounded almost protective. Candy had never felt protected in her whole life, and it was amazingly seductive. But she knew she ought not to agree if she couldn't keep her side of the bargain.

She muttered, 'How would I know what you thought was provocation?'

There was an astonished silence. Then Justin gave a soft laugh. 'Poor Candida. It's not really fair.'

'It's just...'

'I know. It feels like cheating,' Justin said softly.

Candy dipped her head in embarrassment.

'I know what I'm doing. And I know a good deal more about the world than you,' he said. 'Trust me.'

In spite of herself she tensed. She saw him watching the way her knuckles whitened and rapidly straightened her fingers.

Justin went on levelly, 'You don't want less than a proper marriage. Frankly, neither do I.' His smile was wry. 'For all sorts of reasons, some of which you've seen. But I can wait. I'm very good at waiting. But I want a woman, not a child. And I think you need some space.'

Candy was doubtful.

'Let's get married,' he said softly. 'We can take each day as it comes. You'll be away from whatever pressures your parents apply. And I'll—have a sporting chance.'

She sighed. 'I wish I understood you.'

He hesitated. 'You will.'

She gave a shaken little laugh. 'I doubt it. Not as well as you seem to understand me.'

'Well, that's a start,' he said enigmatically.

Candy did not entirely understand that either. She looked at the loose-limbed figure and frowned. Justin was making no attempt to touch her. She realised, with a stab of real panic, that she wanted him to touch her.

She drew back deeper into the security of the chair. Her thoughts were a jumble. But her body seemed to know very clearly what it wanted. It wanted Justin to take her back into his arms.

Candy thought, I must be crazy. I don't even know him.

Yet in his arms she had felt as if she had known him forever. And he had known her. The feelings were shockingly new—but somehow as if she had always, secretly, expected them. And in the last few hours she had let him see more of her feelings than probably anyone else had ever done.

She said, half to herself, 'Everything's happening too fast.'

There was a pause.

Then Justin said in such a normal voice that it made her jump, 'Sleep on it.'

She looked at her watch. She had, she realised, lost all count of time.

'Oh, lord. I must get going.' She jumped to her feet.

He stood up too, uncoiling gracefully. In the shadows he looked very tall. Almost forbidding, thought Candy, backing a little.

'Stay,' he said quietly.

Her heart leaped.

'You're tired and muddled. Don't go home. I can give you a bed.'

Candy stood as still as a statue. Whose bed? What did he want with her?

'Why?' she managed between cold lips.

In the shadows one wicked eyebrow flicked up.

'Your own bed,' he assured her. She could hear the smile in his voice. 'I've made enough mistakes tonight.'

For some reason, that hurt. She bent and picked up her bag.

'No. I'd better go back. My mother listens for me...'

'Your mother will have been asleep hours ago,' he said quietly. He came up to her and put his hands on her shoulders. 'Don't go, Candida. Trust me this much.'

She had the sudden feeling that the decision was momentous, that she was about to set the course for the rest of her life. The hands on her shoulders were strong, but he was not holding her hard. Yet she felt that she would never get away—nor ever want to get away.

She moistened her lips. 'All right.' It was not much more than a whisper.

Justin gave a long sigh as if he had been holding his breath.

But all he said was, 'Good.'

He gave her his own room. She hesitated in the doorway of the pleasant green and gold room, and looked at the big bed, shivering. Justin came up and put an arm round her waist. Candy jumped violently.

'I wasn't thinking of joining you,' Justin said with the first hint of acidity she had heard from him. 'I told you—you've got to trust me.'

'I'm sorry,' she said with difficulty. 'I do—really. It's just that tonight has been—well, a bit of a shock.'

He hugged her briefly. 'And I'm sorry, too. I didn't mean to snap. It's not been quite what I expected either, to be honest.'

Candy hung her head. 'No.'

'Now don't start worrying again. It will work itself out. Believe me,' Justin said firmly. He went to one of the floor-to-ceiling cabinets and extracted a brilliant pyjama jacket in a shiny green material. As he tossed it to her, Candy saw the flash of gold. She caught it and spread it out, holding it by the shoulders. A gold dragon danced across the back.

Justin grimaced. 'A present,' he said excusingly. 'In fact, I'm not sure those Chinese characters on the front don't say "A Present from Shanghai!" It'll be too big for you, of course, but it's all I can think of.'

Candy wondered who had given him that dragon jacket. She turned it over and over in her hands. It would be a woman, of course. Men didn't give each other clothes, especially not those with embroidered heraldic beasts rioting across them. She wondered whether the woman was an old flame, whether her spark still burned.

Justin had said nothing about his other lovers. Other lovers! What was she thinking about? She was not his lover. He had not mentioned love, not once during this whole fraught, frank evening. She did not know what she would do if he did.

He watched the expressions chase themselves over her face and gave a little sigh. She was unaware of it. He came up to her and turned her towards him, mangled jacket and all.

'Don't look like that, Candy. I'll take care of everything.' He feathered a kiss across her eyebrow. 'I promise.'

But he hadn't managed to take care of the loneliness that assailed her in that big, cold bed. He had not even seen it. He had not seen the need in her clutching hands either, though to Candy it had been naked when he'd kissed her a chaste goodnight.

It was a long time before she slept. And when she did she dreamt of Justin and a beautiful Chinese girl running away from her hand in hand while she cried out after them to wait.

The morning was hell. Getting up and padding about his flat as if she were used to staying overnight in the homes of strange men was almost beyond her. Justin, whistling softly between his teeth, seemed completely unaware. Even when she brushed him with her bare arm, reaching past for the coffee-pot, and jumped like a startled cat, he did not notice.

He was in shirt-sleeves but it was clear that he would be his usual self in seconds, shrugging into the superbly cut waistcoat and jacket. Candy looked at him with all the loathing of a sleepless night and at the crumpled jeans that awaited her.

'Don't you ever look untidy?' she complained, taking black coffee to the far end of the breakfast bar.

Justin's eyes gleamed. 'Often. You'll find out when we're married.'

Candy swallowed hard and refused to blush. She gave him one of her better smiles—steady and ironic.

'I look forward to it,' she assured him.

Justin gave a shout of laughter. 'So do I.' He leaned forward as if he were going to kiss her, but did not. Candy, gazing deep into laughing brown eyes, found her breath oddly difficult to keep under control. He knew. She could see that.

Candy's temper rose with her embarrassment. How dared he sit there laughing at her? Just because this was the sort of situation that he was used to and she was not. She glared at him.

'Hadn't you better be going? Won't you be late for work?'

'Very wifely,' he approved, amused. 'But I thought I'd run you home first. I like to see my dates safely to their own doorstep—even if it's the morning after.'

Candy's stomach felt suddenly hollow. Of course there would have been a lot of times when he'd taken a lady home after one of those nights that he had begun to offer her last night and she had rejected so fiercely.

What would it have felt like if she hadn't? Would he have held her this morning? Kissed her? Held her hand while they breakfasted—then taken her back to bed? Or would he have been cool and amused and already putting it behind him while he got ready for work?

I don't think I could bear that, Candy thought, surprised. She stood up sharply. 'No, thank you.'

There was no mistaking her sincerity in the crisp, almost hostile tone. Justin looked quizzical.

'And if I want to?'

'It would be pointless. I brought my own car last night.'

Justin grinned. 'Game, set and match,' he conceded. 'I give in.'

He leaned forward again and this time he did kiss her, a brief, incredibly sensuous brush of his lips and tongue across her lower lip. Candy gasped as if she had been burned. Justin's eyes gleamed.

'You don't know what it's like,' he murmured.

'Wh-what?' she faltered, feeling hot and cold at the same time—feeling a fool.

Justin's smile grew wicked. 'Driving home at this time of day,' he said blandly. He drew a proprietorial finger along her bottom lip and looked pleased when she shut her eyes. 'Hope you don't regret it.'

It was fairly clear that he didn't mean the morning traffic.

He was gone before she could answer. She heard him whistling, sounding disgustingly pleased with himself. Then she heard his light steps running down the stairs, heard him call goodbye as if he did it every morning, and the thump of the closing door.

It was a long time before she stopped shaking enough to scramble into her clothes and set off for home.

When she got to her parents' house it was to find them both in the kitchen while Maria tiptoed between them setting the breakfast table. So Sir Leslie had come back, at least temporarily. Her mother did not look happy about it, though. It was obvious that she had been crying. Candy tried not to think, *again*.

She squared her shoulders and went in.

Her father dropped his paper and glared at her. He was a big man with a fine head of dark hair, now greying, and brilliant eyes. They were now gleaming with an emotion that Candy had no difficulty in recognising. She swallowed hard, reminding herself that she was the only person she knew who wasn't afraid of him. Or not *really* afraid.

'Where the hell have you been?' he asked without greeting.

Candy sat down at the table and poured herself a cup of coffee.

'Morning, Pops,' she said with a calm she was proud of.

'Don't call your father that,' Judith said automatically.

Neither Sir Leslie nor Candy paid any attention to that protest. He flung the paper away from him without making any attempt to fold it properly. Judith began to pick up sheets distractedly. He ignored that too.

'Well? Your mother's been ringing half the country. Seemed to think you'd been mugged.'

Candy was conscience-stricken. 'I'm sorry, Mother.'

'And it's not the first time,' he continued, banging his hand down on the table so that the toast-rack danced on its little spindle feet. 'What the hell are you up to, my girl?'

Candy surveyed him thoughtfully. She was not sure which of her two pieces of news would be the more unwelcome. But there was no point in putting it off any longer. Justin had shown her that.

'I've been helping out at the Homeless Centre. Doing the evening run.'

Sir Leslie stared. 'Homeless Centre? Sounds like some blasted soup kitchen.'

'Yup,' Candy agreed, amused. She picked up an apple and bit into it. 'I've been asked to go on to the staff full time. I want to.'

'Well, you can't,' he said promptly. 'If you want a job you can come into the office. I've told you that before——'

'No, Pops,' she interrupted gently. 'Not just a job. A job I believe in. Where I'm adding a bit to the sum of human happiness, not just making money.'

'You've never had to bother about money,' he said bitterly. She realised with a shock that he sounded exactly like Dave Tresilian. 'You wouldn't be able to play about with down-and-outs if it weren't for my money. What if I stop your allowance?'

Judith made a small, wordless protest.

'Shut up,' Sir Leslie said, not looking at her. 'Well?'

Candy shrugged. 'Then I'll have to find another away to live.'

Sir Leslie's eyes narrowed suddenly. 'What've you been up to? Where were you last night? I don't believe your soup kitchen is open till the morning.'

Candy's heart fluttered. 'No,' she agreed quietly.

His voice sank. He was always at his most dangerous when he was quiet.

'*Tramp*!' It came out with shattering force. 'Don't think you can behave like that and live under my roof. You can get out and stay with whoever you were with last night.'

Candy paled.

Judith said, '*No*. Leslie, be reasonable...'

He rounded on her. 'If you'd been a halfway decent mother instead of always whining and trailing off to health farms, she'd know right from wrong.'

Judith shrank back, white and shaking. Candy felt a cold, pure anger sweep over her.

Her father turned back to her. 'Where were you last night? I suppose it was some man?'

'Oh, yes,' confirmed Candy.

Judith moaned.

'Who?' shouted Sir Leslie.

Candy gave him a faint sweet smile, not unmixed with triumph. 'I spent the night with Justin Richmond,' she said, pleased to be telling the literal truth.

Her mother gave a little wail.

'It's all right, Mother.' Candy added ironically, 'He's going to make an honest woman of me.'

There was a shocked silence.

Then Sir Leslie said furiously, 'You stupid girl.'

Judith said, 'Oh, *Candy*! How could you? He's your father's greatest enemy. How could you let him seduce you?'

Candy shrugged. 'He didn't.'

They misunderstood her, as she'd intended them to. Judith closed her eyes.

Sir Leslie roared. 'It's just to get back at me,' he flung at her. 'He wouldn't care about a child like you.'

Candy flinched at that. But she shrugged again and said calmly, 'Marriage was his idea.'

'Then he's heard about your trust fund,' Sir Leslie concluded rapidly. 'He'd figure that if he could get his hands on those shares in Neilson's it would be a stand off and I'd back away from my bid for Richmonds.'

Candy shook her head. 'I don't think so.'

Judith opened her eyes and stared at her, astonished by the certainty in her tone.

'But darling, you can't be *sure*.'

'Yes, I can. If that's what it was he'd have told me,' Candy said. She took another bite of her apple. 'I trust him and I've given him my word,' she added swiftly. An irrepressible flicker of mirth invaded her eyes. 'So wish me luck and brace yourself to pay for the wedding.'

Justin rang within half an hour.

'You sound all right,' he said. 'How did it go?'

Candy said truthfully, 'My father hit the roof. He thinks you're after me for my shares in Neilson's.'

Justin made a non-committal noise. 'Will he forbid the banns, do you think?' he asked, seeming mildly interested.

For some reason this was more reassuring than any protestations. Candy gave a choke of laughter. 'Not after my mother made it plain I'd been out all night,' she said crisply.

'Ah.' He sounded pleased. 'Persuaded by our night of passion, was he? You must have laid it on a bit thick.'

Candy said with dignity, 'I told the truth.'

'Yes, indeed.' Justin was appreciative. 'I've noticed that before. Do you always?'

Candy said soberly, 'Look, Justin, I don't want you to feel you can't back out, if you want. I know things got a bit heavy last night...'

'Not *unduly* heavy,' he demurred. She could hear the amusement.

'I'm serious. I mean, you might think better of it in the light of day. People do. Once you start to work and your ordinary life takes over, I mean.'

Justin said lightly, 'Nothing could put you out of my mind.'

Candy gritted her teeth. 'I wasn't fishing for false compliments. I was trying to say——'

'Then don't,' Justin interrupted. 'Don't say a thing more. We've got a bargain and we'll both keep it. But it's probably best not discussed. I'll see you tonight.' And he rang off.

It was prophetic, she found. The next days were full of Justin kindly, courteously but quite implacably arranging her life. And refusing to talk.

She had the uneasy feeling that she had lost control of her life. She suspected she was in experienced, powerful hands that were all too used to controlling others.

Of the experience she was left in no doubt. There were plenty of people only too happy to fill in Justin's past for her. Even her mother said unhappily that Justin had known how to get his own way with women since he was a student.

But Lizbeth Lamont was something else. But then Lizbeth Lamont was beautiful and self-assured, and she wasn't talking about Justin's student days.

She sought Candy out at a cocktail party Sir Leslie insisted on the whole family attending. She was a small, dramatic brunette. Her heavily made-up eyes and lashes were tipped with gold.

Judith Neilson took one look at her, as she came bearing down on them, and fled, murmuring incoherent apologies to her daughter.

Lizbeth was wearing a scarlet dress that left her back and shoulders bare. Her fingernails matched her dress. She had a restless manner and a high, tinkling laugh that could be heard across several rooms. She clearly believed in making an impact.

She also believed in coming straight to the point.

'Candy Neilson,' she said thoughtfully, having introduced herself. 'You know, I always thought Leslie would get you in on the editorial side. I never thought he'd let you get into bed with the opposition.'

Candy blinked. Lizbeth Lamont was clearly pleased with the effect of her remark. Impact indeed. It annoyed Candy intensely.

So she gave Lizbeth a wide, cat-like smile and said, 'No, it would be out of character, wouldn't it? Maybe we didn't ask my father.'

Lizbeth's elegant plucked eyebrows snapped together. 'Are you telling me he's serious about you? *Justin*?'

That annoyed Candy even more.

'He seems to be,' she murmured.

'Don't be ridiculous. You're a child.'

And that was not new and altogether too near the bone. She gave Lizbeth Lamont a look of wide-eyed wonder and, carefully, told the truth.

'That's what Justin says.' She allowed her eyes to go dreamy as if she had memories of resonant passion to call on, instead of a series of brisk if kindly instructions. She even managed a blush. 'I suppose he's rediscovering things.'

Lizbeth Lamont looked as if she had rediscovered a caterpillar in her salad and was going to scream, Candy thought with satisfaction.

Behind them, in a voice full of amusement, Justin said, 'I see you two have found each other.'

Lizbeth swung rapidly on her spiked heel and flung herself into his arms. Still clasping him, she turned her head against the shoulder of his impeccable grey suit and gave Candy a look that was pure challenge. She rubbed her cheek against the dark cloth like a cat that expected to be petted.

'Darling. I had to meet the girl who took you away from the rest of us,' she said prettily.

It could have been amusing. It wasn't.

Justin's eyebrows flew up. He put her away from him, as if she had surprised him, and smiled at Candy. It was that warm smile in his eyes which usually turned her bones to water. On this occasion it made her inordinately cross.

But all he said was, 'Well, now you have, I'm going to tear her away. I haven't talked to her myself for much too long.' He took her elbow in a firm grip and steered her away. 'See you around, Liz.'

As she crossed the crowded room on his arm, Candy was seething.

'I suppose you think you're very clever,' she hissed.

He looked down at her, smiling. 'Not very,' he said ruefully. 'Or you wouldn't have had time to meet Lizbeth until——'

'Until I was well and truly under your thumb?' she supplied in a harsh undertone.

Justin looked taken aback. 'That wasn't what I was going to say, no.'

'So what were you going to say?' she challenged mockingly. 'That you're dreadfully sorry and it should never have happened?'

Justin stopped dead. For a moment he looked truly astonished. Then his mouth began to twitch.

'Not at all,' he drawled.

Candy's hand clenched tight round the champagne glass she was still carrying. She had hardly touched it.

'And,' he added swiftly, 'if you're thinking of throwing that thing at me, bear in mind that I arrived after you and mine is fuller. And I believe in retaliation.'

She stared at him. 'You don't mind at all, do you?' she said at last, thinking of Lizbeth curled over him with those sharp little eyes on the fiancée who was no rival.

He watched her carefully. 'Mind what?'

Candy's eyes stung. Perhaps he was even more like her father than she had thought.

'Does it feed your sense of power to see two women spitting over you?' she muttered bitterly.

Justin was quite unruffled. 'Of course not.' He paused. 'But you don't spit, and Lizbeth—though she's perfectly capable of it—has other fish to fry.'

Candy felt outgunned. She was sure there was more to it than that. She was *sure*. But when he looked so bland and open she could not see the holes in his argument.

She said sulkily, 'She was all over you.'

'I'm her employer and she's got a healthy interest in her career. Lizbeth's a woman who never lets slip an opportunity to flatter the influential.'

'And you like it.'

Justin met her eyes steadily. 'I can live without it. I can take your parents treating me as if I have horns and a tail. Though it would be nice if you showed some pleasure in being with me sometimes.' His eyes were suddenly not amused any more.

And Candy, blushing, was silenced.

CHAPTER FIVE

JUSTIN'S family were more welcoming than her own, to Candy's relief. He took her to meet his aunt in a comfortably untidy flat overlooking a Kensington garden square.

'I'm so glad,' Lady Richmond said, kissing her on both cheeks and giving her a hug.

Candy was startled. Her own family touched very little, she realised suddenly. Judith had never yet brought herself to kiss Justin on the cheek. She looked at him. He gave her a bland smile.

'About our engagement,' he said gently. 'That's what Aunt Rose means. *She's* glad for us.' The emphasis was very slight, but it echoed Candy's own thoughts. She blushed.

Lady Richmond waved a hand at him, the other arm still round Candy's waist.

'Justin, don't be provocative. If you will spring surprises on people you must expect some of them to take time to get used to it. Candy knows perfectly well what I mean.' She gave her a little tug. 'Come and sit down, dear, and and tell me—oh, tell me everything. When did you meet? How long have you known each other? Have you fixed a date for the wedding?'

Candy rolled her eyes wildly at Justin, looking for help.

'Er——' she said.

Justin's smile grew. He sat down and crossed one leg over the other, looking interested.

'It was quite—er—sudden,' she muttered. She glared at him.

Kind Lady Richmond was unaware of undercurrents. She beamed at them both impartially.

'I always said when you fell in love you'd fall all at once,' she told Justin with satisfaction. 'Didn't I?'

The brown eyes gleamed. 'You did,' he agreed.

'Dear boy.' Her smile was full of affection. 'And you were so determined you wouldn't. Aren't you glad I was right?'

'Very,' he replied in an amused voice.

It was inexplicably hurtful. Candy bit her lip. Lady Richmond didn't notice. Candy cast Justin an agonised glance which he refused to see. Later, while his aunt was hunting for photograph albums, she protested.

'This is awful. I feel like a criminal. She's so happy for us and we're telling her lies.'

'On the contrary, you told her the exact truth,' Justin said drily. 'A great talent. I've noticed it before. It's one of the things I most admire about you.'

'A sort of half-truth?' Candy demanded with bitterness. 'A few facts and none of the real thing. You admire that?'

He looked at her for a long moment. Then he stood up and came to sit beside her on the sofa.

'Very much.'

He laid one arm casually along the back of the sofa behind her. Candy barely noticed. She turned to him, her eyes filling.

'Look, can't you see? This was what I was afraid of all along about this sort of arrangement. I don't want to tell her lies.'

'You didn't' he said lazily.

Candy was impatient. 'Or let her believe lies.'

He considered her, his head on one side.

'Why?' he asked at last.

'*Why*?' Candy was outraged. 'Because she's so kind. And she's fond of you. I don't want to hurt her.'

He raised an eyebrow. 'And don't you think it would hurt her if you told her that you don't really want to marry me, but I'm the only option you've got?' he asked levelly.

Candy was shocked. 'That's not true.'

'Isn't it?'

'*No*' She turned to him. 'You know it isn't. I——'

Lady Richmond came back into the room. There was no time to say more. Justin didn't move from her side, though he stood up when his aunt came in. And when he sat down again, he dropped his arm casually round Candy's shoulders. She noticed this time, and sat very still.

Oblivious, Lady Richmond chatted. Justin looked down at Candy with a crooked smile.

'Christmas,' said his aunt, holding out a photograph. 'Your first when you came back to England.'

He leaned forward, bringing Candy closer to his body in the casual movement. She could feel the warmth of his thigh pressed hard against her own. She swallowed.

Justin turned the photograph round and handed it to her. 'I look like a bewildered scarecrow,' he said ruefully.

'Well, the family were all new to you,' said his aunt excusingly. 'And there's such a *lot* of family at Christmas.'

Justin chuckled. 'Enough, certainly.'

He named them. Candy tried to concentrate. But she was more conscious of the muscular arm that curved round her.

'I suppose you'll be asking them all to the wedding,' Lady Richmond said happily.

Justin looked down at the photograph. A frown appeared between his brows. He didn't answer.

Lady Richmond didn't appear to notice. She perched on the arm of the sofa and gave them another photograph. She leaned over Candy's shoulder, pointing.

'That the Open Day. Do you remember, Justin? You'd just joined the board, and Henry said it was up to you to be the family's representative in the sack race.'

Justin grinned. 'He also told me not to win.'

He looked up at his aunt. As he did so, Candy thought she felt his lips against her temple. Her eyes flew to his, electrified. But he was exchanging an unreadable look with Lady Richmond. He took the photograph from her and held it for Candy.

'There he is, darling. And that hat has Aunt Rose underneath.' His voice became deliberate. 'And that's Marianne. In the dark glasses.'

'Oh,' said Candy.

She looked at her predecessor. It was a snap, not a posed photograph. But nothing could disguise Marianne Richmond's elegance.

Candy cleared her throat. 'She looks——'

'Panic-stricken,' Lady Richmond said quickly. 'We all were at Open Days. Poor Marianne wasn't much of a joiner-in. And Henry could be a bit of a tyrant.'

Justin handed back the photograph. 'Unlike me.'

His aunt laughed. 'Well, you don't make me run egg-and-spoon races, I'll give you that. But you have a habit of getting what you want.'

All too conscious of the arm around her, Candy shivered. She shifted. The arm tightened.

'You're exaggerating,' Justin told Lady Richmond.

But she wasn't. Candy saw it herself, again and again. Justin seldom argued. He never raised his voice. But, calm and smiling, he got what he wanted—even out of her father.

Sir Leslie's opposition to the marriage was vocal and persistent. It reduced his wife to tears and Candy to white-faced endurance. Justin, walking into a patently vicious exchange a few days later in the Mayfair drawing-room, summed up the situation at a glance and took steps.

'I think,' he told Sir Leslie gently, 'we need to talk about Candy's shares in Neilson's.'

It came as a bolt from the blue. Candy jumped and turned to him in astonishment. But for once he was not looking at her. He was watching her father with a faint smile.

Sir Leslie said, 'You bastard.' He sent Candy a vicious look. 'If you think you're going to use my daughter's shares in my own company....'

Justin said softly, 'They're Candy's shares. She'll do as she wants with them.'

'No, they're not,' retorted her father. 'They're in trust until she's twenty-five.'

Justin looked at him thoughtfully. 'Or until she marries.'

Sir Leslie began to look ugly. 'Are you threatening me?'

Their eyes locked. In the crackling silence, Candy looked from one to the other. She was remembering, coldly, that they were in the same business and her father regarded him as a serious rival. What sort of man was she committing herself to?

Justin said gently, 'Reminding you.'

Without looking at Candy, he reached out and took her hand. She felt the warmth, the strength in his hand. He prised open her clenched fingers and interwined them with his own. Her father's eyes flickered. She knew he had seen the gesture. Perhaps he had been meant to. In spite of the doubt, her hand lay quiescent in Justin's.

'*Not* a terribly good time to bully her, I would suggest. Not when you're relying on her goodwill not to sell those shares. To me, for example,' Justin pointed out sweetly.

Sir Leslie's colour rose. Judith stood up, looking anxious. Justin gave them both his charming smile. Candy saw that it didn't reach his eyes.

'Think about it,' he advised. He glanced down at Candy. 'I'm afraid we haven't really got time for a drink, darling. I booked a table for eight.'

Shaken by the nasty little scene and what it revealed of Justin, she nodded jerkily. 'I'll get my coat.'

He set a brisk pace through the rain-drenched streets. Candy looked at him sideways. Was he as ruthless as her father? As cold and unscrupulous? Or did he just fight fire with fire? She tried to sort out her confused feelings. It was impossible to do at the same time as keeping up with him.

At last he said, 'I didn't realise the way they used you.'

Candy was startled. 'What do you mean?'

'Haven't you noticed?' He sounded angry. 'It's death, getting caught as the pivot between two other people. You keep them apart, so they can't actually close with each other, but you keep them locked together too. You'd be better out of it.' He looked down at her and asked abruptly, 'Do you want the big wedding that your mother's planning?'

Candy blew her nose and put her handkerchief in her pocket. She stared at him.

'What do you mean?'

Justin drew a long breath. 'I mean I don't think you can stand much more of this.' He stopped and turned suddenly, taking her hands between both of his. He looked down at her searchingly. 'Let me get a special licence. Let's get married quickly.'

'But——'

'I want you out of that poisonous house,' Justin said harshly. '*Now*. Marry me soon. Or move in with me.'

Candy gasped. 'But the guests... My mother...'

Justin shook her gently. 'Whose wedding is it?'

She hesitated, searching his face. His eyes were almost black in the dim street-lighting. By some trick of that light, his high cheekbones were illuminated so that he looked fierce and even a little cruel, like a man in pain.

'It matters so much?' Candy asked slowly.

His face changed, became unreadable. He dropped her hands.

'Only if it matters to you. Of course you must have whatever wedding you want.'

Candy made up her mind. She felt shaky but brave.

'You're right. The sooner the better.' She sent him an apologetic glance. 'But you'll have to hold my hand when I tell my mother.'

Justin expelled a long sigh. He shrugged. 'She can still have her party. We just don't put on the performance first. And no speeches,' he added with feeling. 'In fact, the more I think about it, the more attractive the prospect.'

Candy felt as if a great burden she had not known she was carrying had been suddenly taken off her shoulders. She gave him her sudden infectious grin and raised her eyes to the stars.

'Thank you, God, for letting me marry a tough businessman who is also a lateral thinker,' she teased.

Justin stood very still in the shadows. For a moment there was a tension between them which Candy did not understand. She looked at him uncertainly, her smile dying.

Then he gave a sharp nod. Again she had the impression of a man in pain.

'I'll get the licence tomorrow,' he said.

Candy was not on duty at the Homeless Centre that night. She realised that Dave Tresilian was anxious not to provoke either of the powerful men in her life. So he reshuffled the rota. Initially that had hurt. Now, however, it seemed insignificant.

She sat, sleepless, on her bed. She thought of the first night she had met Justin. Was it less than a month ago? Even then, she thought with a superstitious shudder, she had dreamed of him.

What was happening to her? When Justin touched her, she froze, just as she had with Tom Langton. Yet when he didn't touch her all she wanted was to feel his arms round her.

Hugging her arms round her knees, she rested her head against the window-pane. Outside, the rain was teeming down in silvery sheets. The empty street gleamed like a dark mirror. The Georgian houses were dark too. She had never felt so lonely in her life. Nor so out of control.

Oh, lord, if only Justin were here, she thought.

Then she realised what she was thinking. She jumped, gasping aloud. Her hands flew to her cheeks. She could feel the blood burning under her fingers.

How could she want Justin Richmond like that—as if he were the only man in the world she could trust? She must be out of her mind. And if he saw it——

Candy blushed harder. He would be sorry for her. He would see this for what it was—pitiful, childish, naïve. He would probably be quite kind and a little embarrassed.

Either that or he would use it against her, as she had seen him use his knowledge of human nature against others who had opposed him. Candy set her teeth. Out of control she might be, but she wasn't delivering herself up into the power of cool, clever Justin Richmond, she resolved grimly.

She went back to bed. She slept eventually. It was a miserable night. She tossed and turned in the grip of dreams of a mysterious figure just ahead of her in a midnight alley. He was oblivious of her cries for help. Or was she calling out because she was afraid of him and wanted to warn others?

She chased him, and he turned, but she could never make out his face. Twice she awoke, with tears on her face. In the morning, her bedclothes were on the floor and her eyes looked as if she hadn't slept.

Justin saw it at once. He arrived on the doorstep with the morning paper. His eyebrows flew up at the sight of her.

'Problems?'

Candy blinked and straightened her drooping shoulders.

'What are you doing here?'

His answering smile was crooked. 'I've come to solve your problems. Or double them. Depending on how you look at it.'

She closed her eyes. 'Justin, I've had a bad night wrestling with the duvet. I'm not up to riddles. Say what you have to say without the crossword clues—please?'

He reached out and ran a long finger down her cheek, so lightly that he barely touched her. Her skin felt scalded. She jumped. Her eyes came wide awake and she took a step backwards.

'Bad night?' He sounded almost amused.

Candy glared at him. 'You aren't very sympathetic.'

Justin propped himself against the door-jamb and grinned down at her. Something in his eyes made her feel distinctly warm in spite of the spring wind whipping round her bare ankles. She huddled her sensible dark blue dressing-gown closer round her.

'On the contrary,' he murmured.

Candy refused to acknowledge that her colour was rising. He was playing with her, and they both knew it.

'No...riddles,' she said, emphasising the words by thumping her fist against the door-frame.

Justin's smile widened. He took her hand and turned it over to observe the knuckles.

'You'll hurt yourself doing that,' he remarked.

He lifted it to his mouth and touched his lips very softly to each finger. Candy swallowed hard. He looked up quickly and she found he was laughing into her eyes. She began to feel slightly dizzy. He looked satisfied just for a moment. Then his expression became his normal one of casual amusement at the world—or at her, thought Candy dourly.

'Anyway, I've got the licence,' he said lazily.

It was a shock.

'Oh...'

'A bit final?' he murmured after a pause.

'What do you mean?' she said, defensive.

He looked at her for a long moment. Then he shrugged.

'Only that you seem less than delighted. Cold feet, Candy?'

'I never,' said Candy with precision, 'get cold feet.'

Unexpectedly he chuckled. He gave her fingers a quick squeeze before he released them. She glared at him, flexing her crushed fingers, but his expression was bland.

'You astonish me. With this wind and nothing on your feet, I'd have thought you were freezing.'

And before she knew what he was about, he swept her off her feet and into his arms. He hoisted her over his shoulder in a competent fireman's lift, and carried her inside. He kicked the door shut behind him.

'Put me down,' said Candy without much originality but with a great deal of genuine feeling. She could feel his shoulders shaking.

'Certainly.'

He shouldered his way into the kitchen. Maria looked up from the stove. Shock and amusement warred in her expression.

'Good morning,' Justin said cheerfully.

Candy thumped him hard between the shoulder-blades.

'Brute. Bully. Put me *down*.'

He righted her and dropped her unceremoniously on the rug. He was turning away before she had straightened.

'Coffee? Wonderful. You're a marvel, Maria.'

'How dare you?' Candy stormed to his back. 'How *dare* you?'

'Oh, I'll risk Maria's coffee,' he said. 'It didn't kill me last time.'

Maria gave a choke of laughter, quickly suppressed, and passed him a mug of coffee. After one look at Candy's stormy expression, she murmured something indecipherable and eased out of the kitchen. Justin raised one eyebrow.

'I suppose you think you're very funny,' Candy hissed.

Justin considered that, the brown eyes dancing.

'Moderately,' he allowed.

Candy glared. His lips twitched. Driven unbearably, she stamped her foot, stabbing her toe against the leg of the breakfast table. She let out a yell of fury and sank on to a chair, hugging the injured foot to her. The old dressing-gown fell open to reveal her brief cotton nightshirt. Justin looked interested.

Hurriedly she dropped her foot and pulled the worn skirts together over her knees. Justin laughed.

'Get out,' Candy raged at him, rocking backwards and forwards. She did not know how much was pain from the injured toe and how much was embarrassment, but they combined to produce a wholly uncharacteristic loss of temper. 'Go on, say what you came for and get out.'

He put down the coffee-mug and came over to her. Putting a hand over each of her shoulders, he brought the maltreated chair to an abrupt halt. It gave her a strange little flutter in the throat to have him towering over her, so close, so overpowering. She had not realised how tall he was. Her mouth dry, Candy tilted her chin at him defiantly.

'You,' Justin informed her, amused, 'are asking for trouble. I came to tell you the ceremony's fixed. St Luke's. Three days' time. Eleven o'clock.'

'Oh.' The fight went out of her. 'That soon?' she said in a small voice. 'Should I—that is, do I have to tell them?'

Justin looked down at her. His face was almost tender, she thought. Which was ridiculous. It must be a trick of the odd angle at which she was looking up at him.

'Not if you don't want to. We can carry on pretending your mother can organise it all for the moment, and tell them afterwards, if you like.'

'Yes, *please*.'

'You're sure you don't want your parents there?'

He looked at her searchingly. Candy thought of her mother's forebodings, her father's fury. They would try to stop it, she knew. Even now, her mother was going through the motions of making pre-wedding lists, but her attitude made it plain that she did not expect it to come off. At times Candy had hardly expected it herself.

'Quite sure,' she said steadily.

'And no friends?'

Friends? People like Tom Langton and his sister? Or the indifferently charitable, like Dave Tresilian? She swallowed a lump in her throat and shook her head again.

'Very well. I'll arrange everything.' He touched her hair lightly. 'Just don't lose your nerve on me.'

There were sounds of movement on the stairs. Justin straightened at once.

'Time I was off.'

He did not kiss her. Candy noted it desolately. At once she took herself to task for inconsistency. It did not make it any the less hurtful.

As if he sensed something, Justin hesitated. He looked down at her. 'Have dinner with me tonight.' It was an order. 'I'll pick you up at eight.'

He was gone before she could reply. When Judith Neilson came into the kitchen he was already closing the front door behind him.

'Was that Justin?' she asked. 'Maria said he was here.'

'Yes,' muttered Candy.

'I must say, he seems very devoted,' Judith said. She sounded uneasy. 'You won't let him hurt you, will you, darling?'

Candy was startled out of her own thoughts.

'Sorry?'

Judith gave a faintly embarrassed laugh. 'You're such a child sometimes. He's a charmer, I grant you. With a track record to prove it. Oh, darling, are you sure about this marriage? I don't want you to lose your heart just because no one's ever swept you off your feet before.'

'I know what I'm doing,' Candy said carefully.

'You think you do. I wish,' said Judith with unusual force, 'you could see what *he's* doing. He's been cutting a swath through more sophisticated ladies than you for years. Why do you suppose he wants to marry you? It's no coincidence that you're your father's daughter with ten per cent of Neilson's shares in trust. He's a practised heart-throb. Oh, darling, be careful. That man has got you tied up in knots so you can't see straight.'

Candy felt suddenly tired. 'Maybe,' she said. 'But can you see any straighter?'

She got up and left before Judith could answer. But the unpleasant little exchange had done its work. She could not put it out of her mind.

She met him on the doorstep that evening and closed the front door as her mother called out. She took his arm and urged him away from the house.

'Do you always get your own way, Justin?' she asked abruptly.

His brows flew up. 'What brought that on?' he demanded, evidently astonished.

Candy looked him between the eyes. 'The way you—handle me,' she said in a harsh voice.

He looked unforgivably amused. 'But I've been at great pains *not* to handle you,' he pointed out. 'We agreed on it.'

She flushed. 'Maybe that's what I mean.' He drew a sharp breath. Candy swept on, 'You manipulate me, don't you? Sometimes I feel you know something I don't—like some business partner you're taking for a ride. And are going to make a fortune out of.'

She rounded on him and surprised an expression on his face which startled her.

'You're confusing my business ethics with your father's,' he said harshly.

'I'm not. I——'

'Yes, you are. Either that or you've been listening to nonsense about those shares of yours. Look at me, Candy.'

Slightly alarmed, she did. His face was grim. She had a sudden uncomfortable vision of what he must be like as an opponent. At the same time she saw, in a flash of enlightenment, how gentle had been her own treatment at his hands up to now.

He said, 'Do you really think those shares are important?'

She was alarmed. But she was not going to be less than honest in the face of that stern demand.

'I don't know,' she replied truthfully. 'Sometimes it seems ridiculous—like something out of a detective story. I *can't* believe that you would get married for a reason like that. Then I think that this whole thing is completely unbelievable—so why not?'

He said fiercely, 'Give the damn things away.'

'What?'

His eyes were bitter. 'You get them when you marry? Fine. Sign them over to the Homeless Centre as a wedding present to me. Put them into a new trust. Make your father a trustee if you want to. If you trust him.'

She could not bear the bitter look.

'I'd rather trust you,' she said impulsively.

There was a tense silence. Then Justin gave a shaken little laugh.

'Well, don't make me a trustee,' he said at last. 'That would convince your father he's right.'

Candy said in a small voice, 'I'm sorry.'

Justin didn't say that no apology was necessary. He smiled at her, but she could see it was an effort. The shadow was still there.

She went on, 'It was unkind. And unjustified. And bad manners.'

He said lightly, 'Well, I wouldn't have said manners were your strong suit. Not the way you flung me out of the house this morning.'

Candy was grateful. She sent him a look which held a gleam of mischief.

'Until I met you I was the best-behaved girl in the Western hemisphere,' she insisted. 'You seem to make me mad faster than anyone I've ever known.'

Justin managed to look gratified. For a moment she had a twinge of panic. Was this the practised seducer lulling her into acquiescence? Then her sense of humour got the better of her. She tugged at his arm.

'Oh, come on, damn you. Feed me and we'll forget it.'

He raised his eyebrows. But he fell into step beside her.

For the rest of the evening he was a model escort, consulting her preferences, setting her chair, taking the wine from the waiter to fill her glass himself. And all the time his eyes never left her face.

She ran out of bright conversation before the coffee. The tension was almost tangible. Justin was aware of it, she knew, though it did not seem to disturb him as it did her. She cursed her too revealing skin and held her shaking hands in her lap. By the time he drove her home, she was reduced to the silence of profound self-consciousness.

He stopped the car at the end of the quiet street. She looked at him in surprise. The rain had stopped but there was a fine mist; they would get wet in walking back to the house. But she said nothing.

For a moment they sat in the warmth of expensive leather in silence. Then Justin opened his door and swung lithely out of the car. Silently Candy allowed him to help her out of the low-slung seat. His hands were courteous, impersonal almost. There was no reason for the cold little curl of excitement that made her shiver at the brief touch.

He closed the door and locked it, glancing down at her. She began to move towards the house, her high heels loud on the pavement, but he stopped her with a hand on her arm. She looked back enquiringly.

Justin said softly, 'Just one thing.'

She should have seen it coming, but she didn't. He had barely touched her in all the weeks of their engagement. It had never occurred to her that the cool, sophisticated Justin would whip her into a passionate embrace in the middle of a public street under a streetlamp.

And of the passion there was no doubt. Justin was not a schoolboy, and this was no token goodnight kiss. She felt savaged, devoured. It was terrifying. Justin seemed completely unmoved.

He stepped back. Candy put out a hand to steady herself in the reeling world. To her fury it was shaking. She propped herself against the lamp-post and let the comforting anger take over.

'What the hell do you think you're doing?' she rapped. The street was not even empty. In the distance there was a policeman and a man walking a dog on a lead. She was on fire with embarrassment and it made her sharper than she intended. 'You have no right to maul me like that.'

He looked at her thoughtfully. Candy knew that her mouth was swollen and her lips were trembling. It added fuel to her fury. She glared at him in the neon blaze.

Justin was neither embarrassed nor repentant. 'We had a bargain,' he reminded her.

Candy closed her eyes. 'Quite. *I* didn't break it.'

'I think perhaps you did,' he said gently.

Her eyes flew open. 'What?'

His expression was wry. 'I was promised no provocation.'

'Are you saying that *I*... You're crazy,' Candy said with conviction. 'What on earth did I do to make you think...?' For all her brave temper, she was nearly crying.

'You said you weren't happy about my not touching you,' he reminded her gently. He shrugged. 'You can't have it both ways, you know.'

She didn't want to think about that. He was too acute; he had noticed what she was only half aware of herself.

She said hurriedly, 'You misunderstood me.'

Justin did not say anything for a moment. Then, 'Are you sure?'

She didn't answer that, turning away and walking rapidly to the shallow steps that led up to the front door. The black and white squares were lit by the carriage lamp that was generally left on until her father got home. She stopped in the lea of the well-trimmed bay tree in its tub, and turned to Justin.

'I don't know what you're trying to do to me,' she burst out.

Justin put one foot on the bottom step. 'But it isn't so hard to work out,' he said in his most reasonable voice. 'And I thought we might do it together.'

Candy backed, bracing herself against the door.

'Don't.' Her voice cracked.

He shook his head. 'You don't mean that.'

'I do.' She sounded breathless and about thirteen, she thought in disgust, even as her trembling hands pressed against the wood behind her.

'I don't think so. But if you do——' he seemed about to reach for her, but at her instinctive flinching his hands dropped to his side '—then I ought to tear up this licence and stand down St Luke's.' He paused. 'Is that what you want?'

'No.' It was not much more than a whisper, but it was unmistakably sincere. She bit her lip. 'I mean, not unless you want to. Tear it up, I mean. I—oh...' She dashed a hand angrily across her face.

Justin said very gently, 'Candy, I don't think you know what you want.' He came up a step. 'Now, I do know.'

She looked up at that.

'I want you,' he told her evenly. 'As my wife. But not at *any* price. If you don't want the same, then let's say goodbye now. Tonight. I won't pursue you any further. Your parents will be delighted.' His lips twitched. 'And you can go back to being the best-behaved girl in the Western hemisphere.' He looked at her. 'Is that what you want?'

'*No*.' It was strangled and utterly spontaneous.

Justin made a little acknowledging movement of his head, but he said nothing. Candy drew a steadying breath.

'I mean, I've taken the decision,' she said hurriedly. 'I've got used to it. I—can't go back.'

He looked at her steadily.

'I hope not,' he said at last. He went down the steps and turned. 'Eleven o'clock. Thursday. St Luke's,' he said. He hesitated, and then gave her that lop-sided smile. 'Don't let me down,' he added very softly.

Candy stood stone still and watched. He did not turn back. Beating in her brain was the thought that, however clever and manipulative he might be, that had sounded not like an order but a plea.

Two days later Candy got herself into a green dress with dashing yellow satin reveres and cuffs and went to her wedding. She had no hat but she swirled her curls up into an electric tumble on the crown of her head. It made her chin look more pointed and her eyes huge. Normally she didn't wear jewellery, but today she dug out the opal drops her grandmother had given her for her sixteenth birthday and put them in her ears. She was quite pleased with the effect.

She hesitated. Then she dusted a touch of blusher across her pale cheeks and a fingertip of green shadow over her eyes. She turned her head in front of the mirror. She looked, well, not pretty—bony redheads with freckles weren't ever going to look pretty—but quite well groomed and unusually confident.

Candy grinned suddenly at her reflection. 'Getting married must agree with you,' she told it.

She picked up her soft black woollen cloak, delicately frilled at the throat, swung it round her as if she were a bullfighter, and went out to get a taxi to her wedding.

The church was large and echoing. It struck dark as she came in out of the thin sunshine. She couldn't see anything except the high window behind the altar.

For a moment, she stood stock still, attacked by the wildest trepidation: maybe it was the wrong church, the wrong time, the wrong day; maybe Justin had changed his mind, been called away...

Then she heard his voice, warm and close.

'You're here,' Justin said with ineffable satisfaction.

She felt a gentle kiss on her cheek, and found that a small posy of white rose and trailing shamrock had been pushed into her hands. She turned, but he was already a shadow, disappearing down the aisle. Above her head the organ started, unexpectedly. Candy jumped and then, belatedly, realised that Justin must have arranged it. Her eyes were misty as she started down the aisle on her own to join him.

It was a simple ceremony. Presumably that also was at Justin's instigation. But it was beautiful. She had wondered if it would feel furtive and somehow not quite thorough, but it was perfection. She found herself making her vows in a low voice, repeating them in her head. Once she faltered, and felt Justin take her hand in the darkness.

It's going to be all right, she thought, astonished and yet somehow deeply peaceful.

'You may kiss the bride,' said the interested cleric.

Justin touched his lips to hers very gently, and then raised their clasped hands and feathered a kiss across her fingers. Candy stared straight into his eyes as he lifted his head. In the uncertain light he looked almost—reverent, she thought: unusually serious, a little hesitant, very open, as if he was laying his heart bare for her to see. She caught her breath.

At her shoulder she heard the unmistakable sound of a sentimental rush of tears being swallowed. At once Justin's solemnity was banished, and he turned to put his arm round Alison James, the secretary Candy had already met.

'It's all right, Allie. That's the slushy bit over,' he said lightly.

Candy flinched. The flippancy grated. She had been so certain there was something there in the beautiful words. Yet now, in a breath, in a couple of words, he was the cynical sophisticate she knew, who did not care profoundly for anything.

She managed a smile, but it was mechanical. She accepted the congratulations of genuinely moved witnesses, but the magic had gone out of the day. She was quiet through the cheerful lunch party at the Ritz, and only really focused her whole attention on the conversation when she heard a word she recognised.

'*Honeymoon*?' she echoed, sitting up.

'You weren't listening,' said Justin smugly. 'Only a week, I'm afraid. It's all I can manage at the moment. I arranged it. All by myself, too. The arranging, that is. I hope to spend the honeymoon accompanied.'

He grinned at Candy across the table. She swallowed hard and gave him a weak smile in return.

Alison said suspiciously, 'You haven't booked a journey for yourself in years. Why didn't you ask me to do it?'

'Because I have a sense of tradition,' Justin retorted.

Alison laughed and flung up her hands in defeat. 'All right. You're the last romantic man in London, and I'm impressed. Where are you going?'

'Somewhere,' said Justin superbly, 'where you and the board won't find us. As you didn't book it.'

In spite of herself, his humour was infectious. Candy began to laugh. 'You're not romantic,' she accused him at last, when she could speak. 'You're just practical.'

Justin was hurt. 'Can't a man be both?'

She said, almost without a tremor, 'Perhaps. But don't try to con me, Justin Richmond. You're not.'

There was a lurking smile in his eyes. 'One day you'll eat your words,' he promised.

Mrs James, looking from her employer to his new bride, gave a sentimental sigh which startled Candy. Justin looked faintly amused. But Candy was frankly embarrassed when, minutes later, Alison told Paul Summers he didn't want a brandy and they left.

'Have a wonderful honeymoon,' Alison said, going.

Justin stood up courteously. Candy watched with blank eyes. A honeymoon, she thought, the word going round and round in her head like a broken record. How in the world am I going to get through a honeymoon?

CHAPTER SIX

JUSTIN TOOK Candy to a long, rambling stone farmhouse in Provence. It was set on its own hillside which was already ablaze with spring flowers. Candy got out of the car and looked at it doubtfully. It looked very lonely.

Justin watched her, his mouth quirking.

'Don't look so alarmed. We have running water and plenty of wood for fires.'

Candy jumped. 'That wasn't——'

'And you can choose your own bedroom,' he added gently.

'Oh.' She swallowed. She did not know whether she was relieved or hurt. Relieved, she assured herself—on the whole. She made herself meet his eyes. 'Yes, that's what I was thinking,' she said honestly.

He was calm. 'It would be astonishing if you weren't. But there's no need to panic. We've gone at your pace up to now, haven't we?'

She thought in a flash of the heart-stopping glimpse of passion he had afforded her in that unexpected goodnight kiss; of the embrace in his flat; of the way he had swept her into a whole new world of sensation the very first time he kissed her. To say nothing of when she had kissed him. She remembered that smoky dance-floor and her own uncharacteristic behaviour all too vividly. Her pace?

'I'm not sure what my pace is any more,' Candy said ruefully. 'It used to be dead stop. But these days—I don't know; I don't seem to know myself any more.'

'Interesting,' murmured Justin.

Or she thought he did. He was too busy getting cases out of the car for her to be sure.

In the house, however, he was as good as his word. He gave her a pretty panelled room on the first floor with a view of the glimmering valley and the hills behind. She flew to the window with an exclamation of delight. Justin laughed, putting down a small case on a chair.

Candy turned. 'What on earth have you got there?'

Justin grinned. 'Maria is a first-class conspirator. I told her to pack you something warm and comfortable suitable for country walks.'

Candy stared. 'And she just did what you told her? Without even *telling* me?'

'Don't sound so annoyed. She offered to pack some clothes for you.' Justin chuckled. 'Or I'd have had to buy you some, and I wasn't sure you'd care for that.'

There was a long pause while Candy assimilated this.

'You always get your own way, don't you?' she said slowly at last.

He frowned quickly. 'You've said that to me before. Do you really think I bully you?'

'No,' she said. She hesitated. 'Not bully exactly. But you make it impossible for me to do anything except exactly what you want. As if I'm a puppet and you're pulling my strings. I—don't like it, Justin.'

He looked at her for a long minute, his face unreadable. Then he propped himself against the pine dressing-table and crossed his arms.

'And what would you prefer?' he asked in a voice of mild interest.

'Honesty,' she retorted.

His eyebrows rose. 'Honesty, hmm? Plain, up-front, tell-it-like-it-is truth?' There was a faint edge to the smooth voice.

'Yes.'

Candy met his eyes. She realised with a little jolt that she had made a terrible mistake. I'm not ready for this, she thought, taking an involuntary step backwards. She shut her eyes tight as the lounging body came away from the dressing-table with unmistakable purpose.

It was as shattering as before. Yet at the same time it was utterly unlike their previous kisses. It was like being caught in a storm, she thought—blinded and deafened by its violence, aware of nothing but the alien, elemental force of it. Justin, it seemed, had stopped treating her gently.

She was gasping for breath when he lifted his head. He held her strongly. She could feel the rise and fall of his chest as if it were an earthquake. Her head fell back. He stooped, and his mouth was burning on the sensitive skin of her throat.

She made a small frightened noise. He stopped dead.

'That's honesty for you,' Justin muttered against her skin. He sounded angry. He lifted his head and forced her to meet his eyes. 'Still want it?'

Candy was paralysed. Everything she had felt when Tom Langton touched her came flooding back. She felt Justin could read it in her eyes. His fierce, cynical expression hurt.

Then, abruptly, he let her go and turned away.

There was a long silence. She tried to steady her shaking hands.

Justin said quietly, 'What happens, Candy? We touch. You seem to be with me—and then you go away. It's happened every time.' He turned to face her. 'Why?'

'I don't know what you mean,' she said swiftly.

'I don't buy that.'

'We—we don't know each other very well——'

'I know what happens when we touch,' Justin interrupted ruthlessly. His voice gentled. 'Candy, we didn't know each other that first evening. But you came into my arms as if you belonged here. Didn't you?'

She tried to meet his eyes and couldn't. She felt her colour rise.

'Until—until what, Candy? Until I did something? Said something that worried you? What?'

He was waiting for an answer. Eventually she said in a small voice, 'It's not you. It's me.'

His sigh was exasperated. 'It's *both* of us. Something's going badly wrong and I don't know what; if you do, tell me, for God's sake. If not, I'll have to work it out somehow, and then you'll say I've pulled your strings again.'

Candy made a helpless gesture. The dark face softened.

'What is it, Candy? Tell me.'

He sounded almost sad. Staring at him, Candy thought she would never have imagined that cool Justin Richmond could look so tired or sound so vulnerable.

She said impulsively, 'There was—well, is, I suppose— a man.'

Justin's eyes narrowed. She stopped, confused.

'Go on,' he said quietly.

Candy hesitated, looking for the words. What was it about Tom that had frightened her so much? The speed with which he had turned from casual escort into near-violent predator? His physical strength and her own unexpected helplessness in the face of it? The cheerful obliviousness, then and afterwards, to her distress? It didn't seem much in retrospect.

'I was probably very stupid.'

Justin shrugged, his eyes never leaving her face. 'We're all stupid sometimes. *Tell* me.'

Candy took a deep breath. 'Well, someone I knew— and liked, in a way—someone I thought I trusted...' She couldn't go on.

Justin was watching her. 'Seduced you?' he asked calmly.

Candy almost jumped. It sounded so matter-of-fact.

'Oh, no. Not that. We'd been out for the evening and he—sort of jumped on me. Without warning. Or if there was a warning I didn't see it.'

'He frightened you?'

Candy shivered. 'It felt as if he was eating me,' she said involuntarily.

Justin drew a deep sharp breath. But all he said was, 'Nasty.'

Candy shook her head. 'He let me go in the end. He thought I was a bit of a prude, but he did let me go. Well, he didn't want to offend my father, did he? He said . . . he said we'd get married first if I insisted.' She was slightly shaken to hear the bitterness in her own voice.

'Ah,' said Justin, 'I see.' He gave her his most charming smile suddenly. 'And you think, now we're married, I'll think I'm licensed to eat you.'

She flushed brilliantly under the mocking eyes.

'Don't worry,' he told her. 'Eating people isn't my style. What we do, we do together. Or not at all.'

Although he was smiling at her, Candy had the oddest feeling he wasn't really seeing her. His eyes were bleak. She thought suddenly, I've hurt him.

She put out a hand but he was already turning away.

'So not at all,' he said over his shoulder. 'Unless you change your mind.'

After that the week should have been impossible. But Justin was as calm and friendly as if the encounter had never taken place. He did not even avoid personal subjects. Though he took care, Candy noticed, not to touch her.

Candy followed his lead. Eventually, plucking up courage, she asked him about his first wife. He was surprised.

'Marianne? What do you want to know?'

'Oh, what she was like. How long you'd known her, how long you were together, that sort of thing,' she said airily.

And were you in love with her? She didn't say that.

The brown eyes were shrewd. He gave a small shrug but answered equably, 'She was a friend of the family. She wasn't very happy at home and she had an unhappy affair with her boss. My aunt and uncle were very kind when I went to live with them, but my father was seriously ill by then and I suppose I wasn't very happy either. University in a strange country, a whole new, noisy family, a lot of assumptions and expectations that I didn't know how to handle. I was insecure and Marianne was very kind. We were both much too young, of course.'

'A friendly divorce?'

Justin made a face. 'Divorce is a beastly business. I don't suppose it's ever really friendly. I don't think either of us bears ill will, if that's what you mean. A few scars, though. We're polite enough—but we're never going to be friends again.' He sounded sad.

'Did you miss her?'

With a rueful smile he shook his head. 'That's why she left. I was so busy. When my uncle fell ill, there were weeks we hardly saw each other.'

And would you miss me? Probably less. For some reason, it made her feel desolate.

Failing to sleep under the sloping roof, Candy castigated herself for her cowardice. If she had been brave enough to marry Justin, she argued internally, then she should be brave enough to do the thing properly. Yet she couldn't.

It was not that she was afraid of him. Far from it, Candy thought ruefully. Although Justin had not even tried to touch her again, there were times when she longed for him. If she was afraid of anything, it was her own unpredictable response.

When he was away, shopping in the village or on one of his solitary dawn walks, she could tell herself it was all in her imagination. But as soon as she heard his step all her good sense dissolved.

She watched him, largely in secret, all the time. She came to recognise his moods from the way he moved. The set of his shoulders could tell her whether he was tired, tense, irritated. She thought that the week was a greater strain on him than he expected, though any anger was deeply suppressed.

It was a strain on her too. But she hid her muddled feelings from Justin. She was, Candy thought ruefully, good at hiding her feelings. So she was as calm and casual as she could manage. The sleepless nights were the price she paid for it.

It was a relief to go back to London in the end. They went to Justin's flat. He gave her the spare room without so much as a lift of an eyebrow by way of comment. He stood in the doorway, hesitating.

'I'm afraid I'm going to be pretty busy in the next few weeks. What will you do with your days?'

Candy aimed a cheerful smile slightly to the right of the immaculate dark head.

'Move in. Make peace with my mother. Sort out what I do next at the Homeless Centre.'

He looked relieved; or so it seemed to Candy.

'Do you want any help? Moving in, I mean. Or negotiating with your mother.'

Candy shook her head. It would have been heaven. But he had already said he was going to be busy. 'Thanks all the same.'

Justin nodded. Candy felt a twinge of regret. She suppressed it at once.

So Justin, an elegant stranger again in one of his impeccable grey suits, went to the office; and Candy went to the Mayfair house.

Lady Neilson was less reproachful than might have been expected. She had other things on her mind, it was evident. In very few minutes she was confiding to Candy that Sir Leslie had slept at home only once in the intervening week. She attributed this to her daughter's behaviour.

'He's so *angry* about your marrying Justin, darling. He's been horrible ever since Justin phoned.'

Candy bit her lip. 'I'm sorry, Mother.'

Judith's eyes filled with tears. 'How you can... he's such a cold fish. Of course, I know he's supposed to be an absolute lady-killer. But how do you ever know what he's thinking?'

By the way his shoulders lock, his mouth compresses, his eyes go black...

'If it's important,' Candy said quietly, 'he tells me.'

But Judith was not really interested in her new son-in-law. She complained steadily until Candy left with a few soothing, meaningless commiserations and took her cases back to the flat.

She unpacked swiftly, scarcely filling half the wardrobe space. Then she went to the Homeless Centre.

Mel Langham was doing phone duty when she went in. Dave was seeing a journalist and Helen was thumping her way through the correspondence. Candy took up a pile of coffee-stained, dog-eared papers and began to sort through them methodically.

Mel flung a smile at her. 'Thank heaven. Decent filing at last. Don't get married again, Candy.'

Eventually the journalist left. He had a camera, she noticed. Dave walked through the office with him, talking too hard to notice that she was there. The journalist looked dazed.

'Good old Dave. Another half-page spread,' Mel said.

Dave ignored that in a beaming welcome.

'Candy.' He was delighted. He swung her off her typist's chair and into the air as lightly as if she had been a cuddly toy. 'What are you doing here? I thought you were on honeymoon.'

'Done that,' she said breathlessly.

He put her down, still exuberant. 'We've missed you.'

'We told her,' Helen said a little drily.

Candy warmed. 'I thought I'd make myself useful again.'

Dave nodded sagely. 'You'll be useful. We need someone to do some really professional fund-raising.'

Candy, who was signing her name on the evening rota, blinked.

'Dances,' explained Dave airily. 'Royal patrons. Television coverage, that sort of thing. Your husband's on the board of River TV, isn't he?'

Candy went cold.

'I don't discuss business with him, I'm afraid,' she said in a wooden voice.

Mel put in sharply, 'For goodness' sake, Dave, they're newlyweds. They're not going to spend their evenings talking about his *job*.'

Candy flushed scarlet. Dave looked confused.

'I just thought Candy might bring him along one evening,' he said.

Embarrassed, Candy said she would ask. Dave brightened at once but Mel wore a slight frown.

'Look,' she said when Candy was getting ready to go home, 'don't let Dave pull your strings. He does good work, lord knows, but he's a man with an obsession. And he doesn't notice other people too well.'

There was a faint bitterness there. Candy looked enquiring.

'I've had the same crush on him as everyone else,' Mel confirmed in a goaded voice. 'He's that sort of man. Don't fall for that emotional blackmail he hands out. Your marriage is the most important thing now. Go for it.'

It was easier said than done, thought Candy. She had no idea what Justin wanted. And Justin, courteous and as remote as the moon, didn't say.

So she retreated. She spent conscience time with her mother. She worked hard at the Centre, doing the administration in the day and going out on the soup rounds at night. Justin never commented.

So one night she blurted out, 'Justin, is this what you expected when we married?'

Justin stopped in surprise. He had just come in and was in the middle of shrugging himself out of his jacket. He looked very tall, in his tailored trousers and waistcoat. Like some twenties Chicago gambler, Candy thought with a stab of surprise and something else that she did not want to think about. He slipped the links out of his cuffs with great deliberation and shook out the crisp cotton sleeves.

'Well?' insisted Candy.

'I'm not sure I had any expectations,' Justin said carefully. He poured himself a whisky, asking Candy with a gesture if she wanted one too. When she shook her head he came to the fireplace with his drink and looked at her searchingly. 'Did you? Are you disappointed?'

Candy's eyes fell away from his. 'I thought we'd—see a bit more of each other.'

Justin smiled. It could be a trick of the light which made it seem as if the smile did not reach his eyes.

'Is this a complaint about my work schedule? Alison told me you wouldn't put up with it for long.'

'Oh.' Candy flushed vividly. It had not occurred to her that she had the right to say anything about his work scheduling. Clearly his secretary did not agree with her.

Justin watched her wryly.

'You must say what you want, you know.'

Candy decided to be brave.

'All right. I want you to come with me one night.'

He said nothing, watching her over the top of his glass. Candy knew the power of his silences by now. She set her teeth.

'When we're doing the soup run. I just want you to *see...*'

He said nothing for a long minute. He took a long swallow of whisky, not taking his eyes off her.

At last he asked, 'Why?'

Because I want to be with you. Because I want you to know me better. Because I want to know you. Candy floundered through all the possibilities and ended with the weakest.

'Dave said...'

'Ah,' Justin said. He looked down at his whisky. 'Dave Tresilian. The Galahad of the Centre.'

There was note in the even voice that was almost hostile. He could have been talking about an enemy. Candy stared. It almost sounded like—jealousy? But that was preposterous.

'*I* think it's time you saw what I do with my evenings,' she said. 'And why.'

There was a little silence. Justin watched her inscrutably. Then he moved, draining the last of his whisky.

'Very well.' He met her eyes. 'It seems a reasonable idea,' he agreed levelly. 'I'm a reasonable man. I agree. When?'

Candy swallowed. She did not realise how much she had expected him to say no.

Justin extracted a thin diary from the inside pocket of his discarded jacket. He thumbed through it swiftly, frowning. 'Are you going tonight?'

'Yes,' she agreed.

'Then let's get it over with,' he said, throwing the jacket away from him almost violently. 'Tonight.'

It was not a success. After that exchange, Candy thought, she should have known it would not be a success.

To begin with, Dave played it wrong. He was too eager to please, to show off all their achievements. And Justin behaved impeccably, so Dave did not notice the lack of response. But Candy noticed. She writhed inwardly, willing Dave to shut up. But he was on roll and saw nothing wrong.

They all went out in the rickety van together, Dave with his arm casually round her to keep her steady on the bench beside him.

Candy was wearing her usual jeans and sweater, like all the others. Justin, at her insistence, had dressed warmly, in tweed trousers and sweater of softest cashmere under a heavy waxed jacket. He looked hopelessly out of place. His manners were perfect. Only Candy saw that there was an impenetrable wall of ice behind his apparent friendliness.

When they stopped Justin came to her side to start serving out the hot soup and coffee. But Dave was not having that. He wanted to give this new potential patron a conducted tour of the down-and-outs, Candy saw with a sinking heart.

'Dave, don't,' she murmured.

But he chose not to hear. And, with a diamond-hard smile, Justin went with him, his head bent courteously to pick up the monologue. Candy could have screamed.

Dave was still talking when they got back to the van. Justin looked weary. Of course, he had been up since before six, Candy thought with a flash of compassion. And he had looked tired when he'd come in from the office. She felt her irritation with Dave increase.

When they got back to the Centre she was abrupt with him.

'I'd like to show you the projections for this year——' he was saying, but she interrupted.

'We're both tired, Dave,' she told him curtly.

Justin looked down at her, one eyebrow flicking up. Dave looked astounded. She had never used that tone to him before.

'Another time,' Justin said to him pleasantly.

Dave insisted, 'But it won't take a minute.'

'Yes, it will,' said Candy. She softened her words with a smile, but the thread of anger was still there if he cared to listen. 'Once you get going, you forget the time. I want to go home now. I'll see you tomorrow, Dave.'

And she almost dragged Justin back to where they had left the car in the street outside the Centre.

'I'll drive,' he said, holding out his hand for the keys.

It was her car. She had driven them over because she knew the way. She stared at him now.

'Why? You didn't complain about my driving coming here.'

'I thought you were tired,' he said, amused.

Candy bit her lip. 'Not as tired as you,' she replied gruffly. 'Get in. I do this run every night. I can do it in my sleep.'

'Very reassuring,' Justin said drily. But he slid into the passenger seat without argument.

When they got home she muttered, 'I'm sorry. I shouldn't have... Dave sometimes isn't very—subtle.'

'No,' he agreed after a pause. There was an odd note in his voice. 'As you say. How long have you known him?'

Candy thought it over. 'Oh, about eighteen months, I suppose. I met him at the Centre.'

Justin turned his head against the head-rest. She could feel his eyes on her.

'So it wasn't David Tresilian who introduced you to the Homeless Centre?'

Candy shook her head. 'It was one of the nurses who used to come and look after Gran. And then I seemed to be useful, so I kept going back. I didn't really get to know Dave until he came on the run with us one night.'

'He doesn't usually?' Justin's voice was idle.

Candy shook her head. 'He's the administrator. He's there all day. He co-ordinates and mans the phones in the evening.'

'So what was different about this evening?' There was steel in the quiet voice.

Candy shifted uncomfortably. She sent him a sideways look.

'I think you know,' she said drily. She bit her lip. 'Dave sees you as a possible benefactor. You're a rich man—and the Centre is falling apart.' It sounded bleak put like that. A little desperately she added, 'You can't blame him. It's not a glamorous cause. And the problem is getting worse all the time.'

For another long, silent minute Justin did not speak. When he did, what he said astonished her.

'Do you want me to give them money, Candida?'

She looked away, moistening her lips. Did she? She said with care, 'I don't want you to do anything you don't want. Or think is right.'

'But what if I want to do something that *you* don't want?' Justin asked, half under his breath.

She drew a shaky breath. On a panicky note she said, 'I don't understand.'

'Don't you?' All of a sudden he sounded impossibly weary. 'Maybe I'm not thinking straight.' His voice was dry. 'It's been a—full day. Come on, let's get to bed. You must be tired too.'

She was, of course, but it did not mean that she could sleep. She lay awake, turning and turning, pulling the pillows into misshapen bricks round her. She could not get that last disturbing exchange out of her head.

Did he mean that he would support the Centre if she asked him? And, if he did, what did that imply in its turn? Was it a bribe? And if so, what did he want in return?

Candy turned over again, pushing the hair away from her hot face. She was aware of a strange trembling at the thought of the price Justin might want to exact. But if he wanted her, why not say so? Damn the man. He became more difficult to read every day.

But he was no easier in the morning, already dressed and nearly gone by the time she surfaced. He had shadows under the dark eyes. Candy felt guilty about that. But Justin waved away her apologies, kissed her briefly on the cheek, and left.

Another empty day. She went to the Centre in the early afternoon and worked so hard that she could put it out of her mind.

Unusually, Dave came on the rounds that night as well. It was bitterly cold and the bottled gas flame under the hot soup in the van kept flickering. Candy did what she could to keep it warm, but her heart went out to the people she served as they tried to warm their hands round the polystyrene cups.

'Getting worse,' one of them said. He was young, probably not much older than Candy herself, but his rags and stubble of beard made him look ancient. He was shivering all the time.

'Been a mild winter,' remarked one of the others, stoically. 'We been lucky.' He flashed Candy a smile for the bread and cheese she gave him. 'Thanks, ducks.'

'Mild?' echoed the other one disbelievingly.

'This your first year? You wait.'

The younger man shook his head. He looked as if he was going to cry. He took his food and shambled off. His companion looked at Candy and shrugged.

'Pity. Took to drink. Lost his job. Girlfriend kicked him out. He's off the booze now. Can't afford it, can he? But he's not going to get a job looking like that. No address nor nothing.'

Candy was chilled. 'What will happen to him?'

Another shrug. 'Depends how angry he gets. We all get angry after a bit. Most get over it.'

She said, 'And that's it? No hope of anything else?'

He drained his soup. 'Can't afford hope. Gets you hurt.' He put the disposable cup carefully back on the van counter and wandered off, a hand raised in salute.

She tried to talk to Dave about the young man that evening. Dave, however, had other ideas.

'I told you—you can't afford to get involved,' he told her, almost impatient. 'Look, there's something I need to talk to you about. Give me a lift to Kensington. I'll walk from there.'

He had never asked her before. Candy hesitated a second. Then she shrugged and led the way to her car.

He talked non-stop. He wanted her to join the committee. He wanted her to take some training. He wanted...

She stopped the car at the all-night bus stop that was close to the flat.

'Hell,' said Dave Tresilian in the first natural voice she had heard from him all evening, maybe for weeks, 'I want *you*, Candy.'

And he dragged her towards him across the front seat.

For a moment she was paralysed. She could not believe it. A long time ago she had wondered what it would be like to have his love—even dreamed about it. Serves me right, she thought, alienated by the grasping hands, by the need that she did not share. It was like Tom Langton all over again.

She fought herself away from him.

'Dave, please...'

He let her go at once. He said, 'I should have known earlier. I should never have let you go to that cold fish. I should have *realised*...'

'Dave...'

'Was it because I was so blind, Candy? Was that why you married him?'

The awful irony, thought Candy, was that if he had come with her to her mother's party, as she had asked him, she would probably not have been sent off to get rid of Justin. And then wouldn't have had dinner with him, or kissed him or fallen in love... Fallen in love with him? With *Justin*?

She said at random, 'I don't think you've the right to ask that.'

'So you *did*.' It was half triumphant, half a groan. 'Oh, Candy...'

As he lunged for her, she slipped out of the car, slamming the door. It left him looking a little foolish. He stopped. Then, head bowed, he too got out of the car and stood looking down at her.

'I'm not going to leave it like this, you know.' His voice throbbed.

She did not know how to reply. After a moment he stalked with dignity to the bus stop. Candy gave a small gasp and fled for the flat.

Candy let herself in with a sigh of relief. She dropped the tote bag on the floor and leaned back against the closed door, drawing a deep breath. In spite of the warm clothes she was shivering.

Dave's kiss still lingered on her lips. Odd that it had seemed so strange—almost frightening—when she had loved him for so long. She put the back of her gloved hand to her mouth. That too felt strange, as if it were no longer her own. She ran her tongue experimentally round her cold lips. They tasted of the night air.

She heard a sound and her eyes flew to the stairs. At the curve, looking at her over the banisters, was Justin. As their eyes met some odd expression flickered across his face. In spite of her tiredness, Candy came away from the door like a rocket, her spine straightening.

Justin ran lightly down the stairs. His feet made no sound on the carpet. It was, thought Candy swallowing, almost menacing, that swift, silent approach. He stopped on the bottom step and tipped his head on one side.

'Exciting night?' he asked coolly.

For no reason at all that she could think of—he could not have seen that kiss after all—Candy flushed.

'Busy,' she said curtly. 'There seem to be more people on the streets every week.'

'Upsetting for you.' He was watching her.

'Yes.' She bent and picked up the tote bag. It was almost too heavy to lift, and she staggered. 'I'm very tired,' she added.

At once he was beside her, taking it from her nerveless fingers as if it weighed nothing. He looked down into her face, his expression unreadable.

'You don't look tired,' he told her softly. 'You're sizzling with something. Have you been holding hands with the Viking?'

Candy's head went back as if he'd hit her. Her eyes flew to his, unguarded and full of dismay.

'I see,' said Justin, still in that soft, amused tone that she hated. 'Interesting. I hadn't had you down as a cheat.'

Candy winced. 'It's not like that.'

'Then tell me what it's like,' Justin invited. His expression was polite but there was no warmth in his eyes at all.

She cleared her throat. 'It just—happened. I didn't mean to...to...'

'Yes?' he asked unhelpfully.

Her eyes fell. 'Oh—to do anything about it.'

She thought he made a small movement, quickly stilled, as if he'd burnt himself. Candy looked up quickly but he was already in command of himself. She might have imagined it. His gaze was bland.

He said in an even tone, 'You ought to remember, Candida. You promised me no provocation.'

She bit her lip. He must have second sight, she thought wryly. There was nothing to say. Any excuses would only get her deeper into trouble. So she set her teeth and said nothing.

Justin let the silence stretch until she could have cried with tension. She could hear the clock ticking on the landing above them. He did not move.

At last he gave a little shrug and asked, 'Nothing to say?'

Candy gave a small choke of laughter. She knew she was on the edge of hysteria, but even so she was pleased. It sounded as if he did not know how to deal with her. Presumably he was not used to people enduring his silences as she did. It slightly evened the odds between them. If she could withstand that, possibly his strongest weapon, she might yet manage not to be subdued utterly by her clever, manipulative husband.

Justin's eyes narrowed. But he said in a tone of absolute normality. 'Maybe you need a drink. Let's go upstairs and talk about it.'

He gestured for her to precede him. She did, grasping the banisters as she mounted the stairs. She was more tired even than she had realised, Candy thought. The muscles at the back of her calves were screaming. Her very bones felt as if they were made of cement. How could Justin say she did not look tired?

But in the sitting-room he tossed her bag on to a chair and, without asking her what she wanted, poured her a cognac.

'Your coat,' he said, holding out his hand for her jacket.

Candy gave him her jacket. She could not suppress a little superstitious shiver. It felt as if she was surrendering armour of a sort. She was almost certain he saw that.

'Drink your brandy,' he told her.

She raised the glass, grimacing as the pungent stuff hit her throat. He stood over her, watching her.

'Now,' Justin said softly when she had finished, 'I think we'd better rewrite the ground rules here.'

Candy stared at him. He gave a lop-sided smile, taking the balloon glass away from her.

'Don't you want to tell me about the irresistible force?' he mocked. 'You were saying something about not meaning to cheat on me, I think.'

She was shaken by anger suddenly. 'It's not cheating——' she began, but he interrupted.

'No? What would you prefer to call it?' The soft voice was like a whiplash, the contempt undisguised, 'Love?'

His eyes were narrowed. He looked like a dangerous animal on the hunt. But Candy was indignant as well as tired, and the encounter with Dave had shaken her more than she knew. She had got beyond being wise.

'Love? You don't know the meaning of the word,' she flashed.

He drew in a sharp breath. And then he laughed. For no reason at all Candy's blood ran cold. He put down his own glass on the cabinet. The small sound was like an avalanche in the silent room.

'I think you'll find you're wrong,' Justin said quietly.

And, before Candy could move or even think, he took her into a fiercely adult embrace.

CHAPTER SEVEN

CANDY did her best to push him away but he was too strong. Too strong, she realised—and too angry. The immaculate calm had gone, and in its place was something close to a volcano. The change in him was frightening.

She tore her mouth away.

'Let me go.' She was panting.

Justin did not bother to answer. Instead he tipped her back over his arm. She leaned away from him until she thought her back would break, but nothing could gainsay the slow, insolent passage of his mouth down her taut throat.

She put her hands flat against his chest, bracing herself.

'Don't.'

He did not give any sign of hearing her. Through the light cotton of his shirt she could feel his heart. It was racing.

Her heart began to swim. Justin's hands at her waist felt like steel. He was virtually carrying her. His lips were like fire against the exposed skin of her neck. She arched away. The pressure on her spine became excruciating.

Candy made a small sound of distress she was hardly aware of, as her knees buckled. Competently, Justin scooped her up. His mouth did not leave her flesh, but she felt him straighten, turn...

She breathed out, shaking her head to clear it. As the mists dissolved she was dropped unceremoniously. She looked wildly round. She had been deposited in the

115

middle of the great bed she had slept in the first time
she spent the night here.

'Oh, dear lord,' said Candy involuntarily.

Justin looked down at her. His eyes glinted.

'Surprised, Candy? Surely not.'

Mutely, she stared at him. It was only now that she
registered what he was wearing—the crisp shirt with its
uncharacteristic embroidery and the dress trousers told
their own tale. He had discarded the bow-tie along with
his jacket, but still it was obvious. He must have gone
out to some official dinner. Alone?

He was smiling. It was not, she thought, a nice smile.

'I rang. Several times. You must have been at the
Centre for over fourteen hours,' Justin said mildly.

It was a mildness that sent shivers down her spine.
Candy backed into the pillows.

'There was a lot to do.'

She couldn't remember a thing she had done all day,
except for those unpleasant minutes in the car with Dave.
She bit her lip. From his ironic look, Candy suspected
he guessed it.

'Your devotion impresses me,' he said softly.

There was nothing in the gentle voice or the unreadable expression to hint that anything very much at
all had upset him. Candy wondered how she knew that
he was fighting mad. And why it scared her. She shut
her eyes.

With a practised flick of his fingers he unthreaded a
set of cuff-links and shook out the sleeve. It was an ordinary enough gesture, but Candy felt her throat tighten
as if he had shaken his fist at her. She watched the cuff
fall over the supple, long-fingered hand and began to
shake.

'Justin,' she said on a breath.

He sounded like a judge about to give sentence. 'You
look—transparent.' His voice was very level. A second

cuff-link joined the first on the bedside table. 'Only, you tell the truth so it works like a lie. And you don't— quite—cheat because you don't—quite—promise what you seem to have promised.' He shook his head at her. 'It's clever, but it won't do, my dear. You have to play the same rules as the rest of us in the end.'

The savage note in the quiet voice was unmistakable now. He was unbuttoning the shirt, his fingers clumsy. Candy had never seen him clumsy before. He did not take his eyes off her white face.

'It's a shame. I thought you were different. More fool me.'

He threw the shirt away from him with a movement that was a declaration of battle. Candy went cold. He put one knee on the bed and leaned forward. She closed her eyes rapidly against that glittering scrutiny.

'You don't look like a cheat,' he mused. 'But then, you don't look very married either. We must change that.'

She gasped. But it was lost in the hot frenzy of his kiss.

There was a brief, violent interlude while he wrenched her out of her clothes. Candy was shivering so much that she barely fought him. She was horrified by the storm she seemed to have unleashed.

That Justin—cool, self-possessed Justin—could strip her with this cold ferocity was horrible. She had never seen him anything but in control before. He would hate being reduced to this, she knew. There was no trace of his normal courtesy. No chivalry. He treated her—looked at her—as if she were his enemy. As if he despised her. Candy fought back in panic, her mind racing. When he calmed down and looked back on this, he would be appalled, she realised.

She began to struggle then. Too late. They were both naked and Justin's eyes were alight with a devil's laughter.

Candy tried to hide the shakiness of her voice. 'Look,' she said, trying for a reasonable tone, 'you'll regret this, you know.'

Justin had one hand on each of her arms, holding her down easily, watching her. He shook the hair out of his eyes.

I've never really seen him with his hair disarranged before, Candy thought with a pang.

He laughed down at her, his face full of that dark and secret amusement.

'I doubt it.'

The tanned, taut skin, so unlike her own, was hot. She felt his closeness would suffocate her. Candy turned her face away, her breath coming unevenly. She tried not to look, but the bunched muscles in his shoulders spoke uncompromisingly of a strength she had never even thought about.

The dark head bent, and he kissed her lingeringly. Her whole body jerked in astonished protest.

He laughed again. There was almost a reckless note in it. Candy stared up at him, frozen. His body moved against hers, explicitly. Candy gasped. She felt the blood rush into her face. In an agony of embarrassment she screwed her eyes tight shut.

What was worse even than the super-cool Justin in this naked fury was the way her body was reacting. Even without kindness or chivalry or any sign of affection, her body responded to him, savouring the harsh caress as if she were a stroked cat. It appalled her. What sort of woman was she?

Justin rolled away so that he was lying beside her, his hand sweeping over her very lightly and slowly. Candy could feel his eyes on her. She set her teeth, horrified at the sensations he was evoking. The trembling started deep in the core of her. His mouth touched her skin, softly, randomly, until she was screaming silently for more. Eventually she could bear it no longer. As he raised his head from a long, deceptively tender kiss, she reached for him.

His breath caught and he moved over her. Candy's thoughts were spinning round on a crazy wheel: I must be mad; I don't know what to do; he'll be so angry; *I want him.* And then he touched her in a new way, and the wheel span off into outer space.

Darkness with dancing lights beyond and great imprisoning walls closing her in. Her heart was racing so hard it hurt. She knew she was in deadly danger. Out of the blackness a figure came stalking silently towards her. She tried to press herself back into the wall, not sure if it was friend or foe, but horribly afraid. A waterfall cascaded somewhere behind her. She was so alone, so vulnerable.

Candy fought her way out of sleep, her heart still crashing. Hell, she thought, what on earth was I drinking last night?

And then the water was shut off and the door opened and closed with a dull thud that was altogether too close for comfort. Cautiously Candy opened her eyes. And then jackknifed up on the pillows in horror.

Justin, in a shabby brown robe, was towelling his hair. He had all too obviously just come from the shower. He was watching her. In one comprehensive glance, Candy registered where she was and how she'd come there. Her hands came up to cover her mouth like a small child holding in a cry of shock.

She dared a look at him. Justin's mouth was wry. He didn't seem any happier to have her there than she was to be there, Candy thought.

But the cool sophisticate was back this morning. He flicked his fingers through the scarcely dry hair and folded the towel neatly lengthways. Then he dropped it over a radiator. 'Good morning,' he said calmly.

Candy knew she was blushing. It did not help that he had the protection of his robe while she was very conscious of her nudity under the covers. She took what she hoped was unobtrusive hold of the sheet and anchored it firmly under her arms.

'G-good morning,' she said in a small voice.

There was wintry amusement in the dark eyes observing her manoeuvre. But he did not comment on it. At least he had that much chivalry left, Candy thought, resentment beginning to rise again.

'Did you sleep well?' His voice was bland.

Candy glared at him. For a moment their eyes met and held. Then Justin turned away with a small shrug.

He was going through one of the wardrobes at the end of the room. He said casually over his shoulder, 'I'm late.'

Candy looked instinctively at her wrist. Then, blushing, remembered that Justin had not even permitted her to keep on her wristwatch last night. She remembered how he had kissed all the way round her wrist as he'd peeled the simple leather strap away.

She watched him under her lashes. Now he was selecting shirt and suit and tie and socks with all the speed and efficiency of a man who woke up every morning with a rumpled and seething wife in his bed. She could cheerfully have thrown something at him. Surely he could say *something* about what had happened?

But he said nothing, dressing with an unembarrassed rapidity that made it very obvious that waking up with *someone* in his bed was a fairly ordinary experience for him. Candy found all her anger left her abruptly, leaving her feeling bleak.

But she still had her pride.

Lifting her chin, she said, 'I'm sorry you're late.'

Justin turned, one of those wicked eyebrows flicking up. 'Are you?' He sounded amused.

Candy refused to think about the desolation inside her.

'If you don't need that robe any more, perhaps you'd let me borrow it. Just for this morning,' she added with some emphasis.

Justin had raised his hand to toss the robe to her. At the rider he hesitated. Then his mouth quirked and he lobbed the thing across to her.

'Of course,' he said smoothly.

He watched unashamedly as she got up. Candy abandoned as soon as it was born the idea of huddling into his robe under cover of the sheets. That would only increase his hateful amusement.

So she got unhurriedly out of bed, meeting his eyes proudly as she slipped her arms into the robe. He made a little movement of his head, as if acknowledging her defiance for what it was. Then he turned and went out.

Candy sagged against the side of the bed in relief. She realised that her body was stiff and slightly hollow-feeling. She rotated her shoulder experimentally and winced. She and Justin had not been gentle with each other last night, she thought.

She went over to the mirror on the inside of the cupboard door and slipped the robe off her shoulder. Yes, unmistakable on the pale skin of arm and shoulder-blade was a bruise.

There was a small sound behind her. Candy turned.

Justin was standing in the doorway. He was holding a mug of coffee. The aroma wafted across to her. He was looking at the image in the mirror. His eyes were very dark and without expression.

But all he said was, 'Battle-scars?'

Candy flinched from the casual callousness of that. For a moment she hated him with a ferocity she hadn't felt since childhood. She pulled the robe back up round her throat and closed the cupboard door sharply.

'Don't you care if you hurt me?' she asked in spite of herself.

Justin put the coffee down carefully.

'Did I?'

Candy shivered. *You'll never know how much.* She didn't say it. But Justin saw the movement and was quick to interpret.

'I'm sorry if I was a little—enthusiastic.' He didn't sound sorry in the least. 'You should have told me it was your first time.'

Candy gave a little laugh that broke in the middle. She picked up the coffee-mug and dipped her nose in it.

'It wasn't very easy to tell you anything last night,' she pointed out.

'Oh, I don't know. We had quite a conversation, one way and another. You had plenty of time to hand over the information that you were a virgin. If you wanted to.' Justin looked very cynical. 'But maybe you thought it would be a useful weapon to level at me this morning.'

He put his hand on her shoulder and turned her round, coffee-cup and all, to face him.

'Forget it, darling,' he said softly. 'You've been playing with fire for weeks. And you know it. And now you know that I know it too, maybe you'll behave a bit better.'

Candy was rigid. His eyes were like black ice. There was none of that illusory tenderness that had seemed to be there, in the end, last night. The hurt was like a burn in her throat.

She forced herself to drink some coffee calmly. Then she put the mug down, shrugged his hands off her shoulders and turned a cool face to him.

'How clever of you, Justin,' she said. 'I will, of course, do anything to avoid a repetition of last night.'

Just for a moment she thought she had succeeded in getting to him. His head went back as if at a blow. But when she looked into his eyes she could see that he was laughing.

'Then we understand each other,' he replied smoothly.

He drew the back of his hand down her cheek. Candy stood absolutely still. Her eyes narrowed to slits with the effort of keeping back the pain that overwhelmed her at that insolent caress.

She said sweetly, 'Do that again and I'll throw this excellent coffee all down that fancy waistcoat of yours.'

His eyes lit up with unmistakable laughter. He bent and feathered the lightest of kisses across her outraged lips.

'That would be a pity. Especially as it's only just escaped champagne this morning.'

Candy stared. 'Champagne...?'

Justin laughed and kissed her again, his breath achingly familiar against her parted lips.

'Think about it,' he advised.

And was gone.

It did not need a lot of reflection, after all. He had indeed opened a bottle of champagne. Jeremy was sipping at a tall glass when Candy went into the kitchen. Jeremy was an aspiring ballet dancer who paid for his training by doing housework. Up till then Candy had regarded him as a fellow spirit.

Now she looked at the other glass on the draining-board and felt as if the whole masculine world was in league against her. She banged the mug down on the counter-top. Jeremy picked it up composedly and rinsed it under the hot tap.

She said between her teeth, 'If you say anything—just one word—about my private life, I'll turn you off without a reference.'

Jeremy shook his head sadly. 'Oh, the power of the capitalist.' But he was grinning. 'Does that mean you don't want any fizz?'

Candy looked at him haughtily. 'Why should it?'

'Well, Justin was celebrating this morning, but you seem a bit less than festive,' Jeremy said frankly.

Candy toyed with the idea of screaming until the ceiling fell in, and abandoned it. Jeremy wouldn't care, and Justin, who was really responsible, wasn't there. If he had been, he probably wouldn't care either. He might even, she thought, remembering that diabolic laughter, enjoy it.

Jeremy patted her on the shoulder, not unsympathetically.

'You'll be all right,' he assured her comfortably. 'You couldn't have gone on as you were. But you'll be all right with Justin. He's a good man.'

And Candy found a glass of champagne pushed into her clenched fist. She choked, half laughing, half in tears. Jeremy raised his glass to her solemnly. She hesitated, then, shrugging, drank it down.

Jeremy looked at her curiously over the top of his glass.

'Going to start changing things?' he asked mildly.

Candy stared. 'Changing things?'

He grinned. 'Throwing out the old curtains. Making cushion covers. That's what they usually do. Nest-building.'

'They?'

'The ones who thought they fancied being Mrs Richmond, I suppose. Well, Liz Lamont, anyway.'

'Oh.'

Candy paled. She looked down into her drink. Liz Lamont was beautiful and poised and a success in Justin's world. If she had stayed here last night, Justin would have wanted her for herself, not her strategic shareholding or her family connections.

If only last night had been different, Candy thought achingly; if Justin had made love to her because he wanted to, instead of because he was in a furious temper, if they had woken up friends... But that was all a dream. Justin had not wanted her last night and he did not want her this morning. He had been angry, nothing more.

And in that anger he had revealed to her what she must have been running away from in her head for weeks—the fact that she wanted him quite desperately. Candy's head fell lower as she thought about it. She wanted to be in his arms; she wanted him to respond to her as she had responded last night, without reserve or hesitation; but, more than that, she wanted his friendship and his trust.

His love. That was what she wanted. She had been blind. She was in love with Justin.

She must have realised it last night when Dave was kissing her. Her mouth quirked. Not the best time for realising you were in love with your husband, she acknowledged.

Jeremy looked worried.

'Look, don't get the wrong idea. They work together and she's a very managing lady. They may have had a bit of a fling at one time, but it must have been long ago. I haven't seen her here for months.'

Candy smiled wryly. 'It doesn't matter.'

If anything, that deepened Jeremy's look of anxiety. But all he said was, 'If you say so. No furniture-moving today, then?'

She shook her head.

'OK. Up to you, love. I'll get on with the polishing, then. You let me know if you change your mind.'

And he went whistling off through the flat.

Candy knew that she could not take sitting and listening to Jeremy's tuneful housework. She scrambled into her clothes and left him to it, with a brief announcement that she didn't know when she'd be back.

Her mother was in her pretty boudoir when she arrived. She looked up at once and smiled.

'Hello, darling. You're looking pretty done-up,' Judith said frankly. 'As if you need to go through the night again.'

Candy repressed a shudder. *Again*? And yet her treacherous body warmed at the thought of some of the things they had done last night. But then this morning Justin had walked out as if it meant nothing. No, she could not take another night like that.

Judith's eyebrows rose. 'Problems?'

'Nothing I shouldn't have seen coming,' Candy replied on a sudden spurt of bitterness.

'What you need is a morning's shopping and a civilised lunch,' Judith said hastily—before Candy could tell her details, her daughter thought wryly.

Candy gave a little laugh which broke in the middle. It was Judith's own unfailing remedy when Sir Leslie left home. Candy did not think it would do much for her own state of mind, but she felt too worn out to protest.

Judith swept her through the smart dress shops that enjoyed her patronage with enthusiasm. Candy deflected all attempts to make her buy something she had no use for. She stayed immune to accusations that she was letting Justin down by looking so scruffy. But she was frankly grateful when they arrived at the small expensive restaurant that Judith favoured.

She couldn't concentrate on the food, however. She ordered at random and ate so little of the delicious food that Judith was anxious.

'Darling, there's no point in starving yourself. You'll make yourself ill and then where will you be? Men can't *abide* illness and fusses.'

Candy pushed her plate away.

'You're probably right. I'm just not hungry.'

Lady Neilson's eyes narrowed. 'You're not having a baby?'

Candy went scarlet. Her mother surveyed her for a long moment and then put down her own knife and fork.

'What have you been up to, Candy?' she asked apprehensively.

Candy shook her head. 'Nothing.'

'Oh, yes, you have. You looked just then exactly as you used to when Nanny caught you playing with your father's briefcase.'

'You're imagining it.'

Lady Neilson rested her elbows on the table and put her elegantly manicured fingertips together in a steeple.

'There are times when you can be amazingly irritating,' she said pleasantly. 'If you've been trailing that long face and those disgraceful jeans round Justin's home—no doubt moaning about the disadvantaged at the same time—I'm not surprised if you've driven him to the end of his tether. Is that what happened?'

Was that what last night was? The end of Justin's patience?

Candy flushed. 'He hasn't asked me to stop going to the Homeless Centre,' she began evasively.

Lady Neilson did not notice the evasion. 'And how much time have you been spending there?'

'Well—er——'

'Running away,' said Lady Neilson with maternal frankness. 'That's what you've been doing. He's too grown-up for you, that's the trouble. So you've dived back into that bunch of students and drop-outs and pushed your husband away. Haven't you?'

Candy said hotly, 'It isn't like that...'

But Judith was unheeding. 'I don't suppose he knew whether he was on his head or his heels, poor chap. He must have thought he was getting a reasonably civilised wife who'd entertain for him and make him comfortable, and look at you—dressing like Orphan Annie and behaving like an adolescent. If he lost his temper, I don't blame him.'

'Thank you very much for your support,' Candy said grimly.

Judith looked startled for a moment. Then she laughed.

'I don't mean to be unsympathetic, darling. But you must grow up a little. You can't treat a man like Justin as if he were one of your soup-kitchen cronies, you know. He's used to certain standards—not least of behaviour.'

Candy thought of the behaviour Justin had demonstrated last night, and laughed harshly.

'He is,' she agreed.

Judith obviously did not like the laugh or the expression on Candy's face.

She said uneasily, 'If he's said something... I'm sure there'll be a reason...'

'Oh, there will,' agreed Candy. 'Justin never does anything without a reason.' She added almost to herself, 'And there'll certainly be a reason for—last night.'

Judith looked even more uncomfortable. She leaned forward.

'Darling, marriage is a very difficult relationship. It's up to the woman to make sure that it stays on the road. Men get out and about so much more. The temptations... We have to do what we can to make sure that they're not tempted...'

She trailed off. Candy was looking at her in undisguised disgust. But it was not Candy's scornful expression, or the outdated sexism of her own argument that brought the look of blank horror into Judith Neilson's face. She stiffened.

'Isn't that——?' she said and stopped abruptly.

Candy looked round without interest. In the corner a dark man was holding a chair for his companion. She looked up, placing a proprietorial hand briefly against his jacket. It was the possessive brunette in the red dress: Lizbeth Lamont. Candy shrugged.

But as the woman's escort turned to take his own seat, Candy's heart squeezed. The elegance, the cool sweep of dark hair were unmistakable. It was Justin.

He had his back to her. Lizbeth sat opposite him, clearly absorbed in her companion. Candy watched the lovely, troubled face and tried to tell herself there was no reason why Justin should not lunch with one of his employees.

It was not much use. It did not look like a business meeting. Neither of them was pretending that their earnest conversation was anything other than personal. They were engrossed in each other. Lizbeth looked tired and strained. Justin touched her hand comfortingly. She was talking as if she couldn't stop.

Forgetting her own companion, Candy strained her ears.

'I need you to understand.' Lizbeth's voice rose in her agitation. '*Please* understand, Justin.'

He looked worried. He murmured something, leaning towards her. Evidently Lizbeth didn't find it soothing.

'I can't go on like this.' Her voice spiralled. 'I don't care what you say. I can't.'

It hit Candy like a blow in the stomach. Her head went back. She made to rise, to go over to their table, when Lizbeth's next announcement pinned her to her seat.

'Nothing must hurt *her*,' Lizbeth hissed. '*She's* so frail. *She's* so vulnerable. What about me? Don't I count? Doesn't it matter if *I* get hurt?'

Justin took her hands and held them between his own on the table. It was a tender gesture. He seemed to be trying to reassure her. But Lizbeth shook her head and glared at him.

'You're all the same. You think a career woman is cast iron. We can take anything you hand out. It's not *fair*.'

She sounded fierce. But Candy could see the tears in her eyes.

CHAPTER EIGHT

LIZBETH could just have been confiding her problems in an old friend, of course. Candy told herself that over and again throughout the rest of the day.

But she could not forget the look on her mother's face. Judith Neilson was an expert on two-timing husbands, and she had looked as if she had uncovered a disaster. She denied it, of course. She did not admit to having overheard any of that revealing conversation either. But she could hardly wait to pay the bill and leave.

Candy went to the Centre and flung herself into filing and typing. Judith had protested mechanically at the decision, but had not really tried to dissuade her. She'd said she had a headache and was going home to nurse it. She'd certainly looked ill, Candy thought.

Candy herself was trying to ignore an uneasy feeling that crisis was approaching. She did not even notice Dave's slight self-consciousness when he perched on the corner of her desk. And every time the telephone rang she jumped in case it was Justin. It never was.

She went home eventually when there was nothing else to do and the evening group were beginning to arrive. She went reluctantly, negotiating the Underground in a sort of daze.

Her preoccupation ended abruptly when she reached the flat. From the drawing-room, a solo violin was pouring passionate lamentation into the night. So Justin was home. Candy hesitated.

She did not want to face him. There was too much between them: the astonishing, undisciplined passion of the night before, the morning's sophisticated indifference—and now that meeting with Lizbeth which she had so unwillingly witnessed.

Candy squared her shoulders. There was something to be faced and nothing to be gained by putting it off. She went resolutely into the sitting-room.

Justin was not sitting in the armchair as she had expected. She knew the pose so well, head tipped back against the cushions, eyes closed as he listened to the music. She had crept around him so often as he listened.

But this time he was standing in front of the window. He had discarded his jacket. The dark waistcoat and slim trousers skimmed his lean length, making him look impossibly tall. He was looking out into the street. In his right hand he held a violin.

Candy stopped dead, all her confused thoughts flying out of her head.

'That was *you*?' she blurted out.

Justin swung neatly round. His face was in shadow, but she had the feeling that he had slipped a mask into place.

'Yes,' he said indifferently.

She came further into the room. As she watched he bent and opened the violin case, putting the instrument away with care. Candy watched, fascinated by the deft movements. She remembered the way those long, sensitive fingers had touched her skin last night. A deep inner trembling began.

She cleared her throat and said too loudly, 'I haven't heard you play before.'

Justin gave her a quick, unreadable look. But all he said was, 'No, I've been neglecting it.'

It was an excuse to talk about anything but last night. Candy seized it eagerly.

'Have you always played the violin?'

It sounded stupid, the sort of question a nervous schoolgirl asked a new acquaintance. To achieve the sound she had heard he must have been playing all his life. She bit her lip miserably.

He watched her, eyes narrowed. But he answered icily, 'From the age of three. My mother thought I ought to play an instrument as insurance.'

'Insurance?' Candy echoed blankly.

He shrugged. 'Where my mother came from there wasn't much in the way of education. Or job security, for that matter. Her view was that a man who can play the fiddle can always earn a crust somewhere.'

'Where your mother came from?'

He looked at her levelly. 'She's Magda Steinitz. The opera singer. Didn't you know?'

Candy was chilled. Here was further evidence, if she needed it, of how little she knew about him.

'No,' she said with constraint. 'When you took me to meet your aunt, I sort of assumed that you were an orphan.'

Justin laughed. 'Oh, Magda's alive all right. You'll meet her one day.'

'You didn't want her at the wedding?' Candy asked with an effort, trying to banish the hurt from her voice.

'She's not that sort of mother.' He hesitated. 'She has a very demanding career. They book themselves up years in advance. She and my father broke up when I was a child. Long before I came to live in England. I hardly saw her. We're quite good friends but...' he shrugged again '...you can't pretend an intimacy that isn't there.'

It sounded amazingly cold. Candy clasped her arms round herself.

'Your father?' she asked after a moment.

'He was a philosopher so he was bit of a wanderer too. He taught at various universities in Europe and the States. He died. In the end he was worn out, I think.'

The handsome face was grim with memories. Suddenly he didn't look cold so much as hurt.

She asked, 'Was he trying to keep up with her?'

His mouth twisted into a hard line. 'With Magda? Maybe. He never accepted that she'd really gone. He was always getting ready for her to come back.'

Candy had a quick vision of the boy trying to make his clever, obsessive father realise that the idolised mother wasn't going to return.

She said gently, 'It wasn't your fault.'

Justin sent her an impatient look. 'Of course not. Any more than your parents' problems are yours. That doesn't stop you running round after your mother, does it?'

Candy winced. It wasn't so far from what she'd thought herself more than once. That didn't make it any more acceptable from Justin.

She said coldly, 'She needs me.'

He was unabashed. 'Perhaps. What of other people's needs? Or even your own?'

For no reason at all, her hands began to shake. She put them swiftly behind her back before he could see it and draw the wrong conclusions. After last night he would have some justification for believing that that deceptively soft note in his voice could make her shake. She searched his face. It was expressionless. As usual.

'Shall we have a drink?' she asked, with a brightness that sounded horribly contrived even to her.

She would not have blamed Justin if he had exploded at the falseness. But he did not. He ignored it.

He said steadily, 'You aren't going to forgive, are you, Candy?'

That threw her.

'Forgive?'

'My ungovernable lusts,' Justin explained with precision.

'*Oh.*'

It took her utterly by surprise. She could feel the hot colour flooding up under her fine skin. The consciousness of it made her blush harder. She pressed her hands to her burning cheeks, her eyes daring him to mock. But Justin's cool expression did not waver.

There was another of those terrible silences. Candy fought for composure, for something—anything—to say that would take them back to a civilised exchange. But all she was aware of was the jumble of shameful emotions she had experienced seeing him with Lizbeth—the deadly accuracy with which Justin had deduced that Dave had kissed her, the whole gamut of feeling she had experienced in his arms last night, her own realisation this morning that she loved him and wanted his love. Above all that she wanted his love. None of that was in the least civilised.

She turned her burning face away.

'I can't—talk about it.'

He said something under his breath. She was not sure what. She tensed. And then the telephone began to ring.

Candy jumped and made an instinctive move to answer it. Justin caught her hands.

'Let it ring.' His voice was unexpectedly urgent. 'Candy, you must see—this can't go on—I—damn, why doesn't the blasted machine answer?'

'I forgot to set it,' she said, tearing herself away. 'It's my fault. I'm sorry. I must...'

And she fled from him to the far end of the room, turning her back on his expression. The furious frustration that she had glimpsed had to be an illusion, she thought, answering the telephone at random.

It was her mother. She sounded desperate. Candy listened with half an ear, aware of Justin's silent presence behind her. Candy kept her back firmly turned.

'Your father's bought her a house in the country. This is the end,' Judith was saying. 'I simply can't bear any more.'

It was a familiar refrain. But for once Candy did not feel responsible. She felt she had no room for feelings about anyone else at that moment. Ears stretched for Justin's every movement, she answered mechanically.

'Oh, darling, he was *unspeakable* last night. You don't know how *glad* I am that you're married to Justin and out of it.'

'Yes,' said Candy hollowly.

Behind her there were small rustling movements as if Justin were picking up papers or—her throat dried—getting undressed.

'I suppose you haven't seen him, today, Candy? I couldn't get him at the office, and from something that cat of a secretary said I thought he might be with you,' Judith was babbling.

Candy was startled. 'Who, Mother? Justin?'

The movements stopped.

'Your father. Has he told you...?'

'No.'

Judith did not even attempt to disguise her disappointment.

'Would you—I mean, do you think you can talk to him, darling? I mean—just find out what he's going to *do*. About the house and me and everything.'

The door was being opened. Candy swung round. Justin stood there for a moment, watching her broodingly. He had resumed his jacket. His handsome face looked suddenly harsh, as if he were going into battle. Their eyes met. Something tugged at her heart and she reached a hand out to him. But he had already turned away.

'Could you, darling? Please? I'll never ask again,' Judith said in her ear.

The door closed behind him. Involuntarily Candy stepped forward, then paused, looking at the telephone in frustration. In the distance, the front door closed with a thunk. It was like a coffin lid closing, she thought.

On the other end of the telephone Judith was becoming hysterical.

'Candy, you've got to help me. You've *got* to. He'll listen to you...'

For the first time in her life, Candy withstood that appeal.

'Pop has never listened to me in his life, Mother,' she said wearily. 'You know it as well as I do.'

Taking the telephone with her, she went to the long window, pushing aside the heavy brocade curtain to see out into the street. From the entrance to the underground garage, the nose of Justin's Mercedes emerged.

Candy flattened herself against the window, trying to catch his attention. But he did not look up. Or at least not until he was in the stream of traffic and waiting at the traffic-lights. And even then she could not be sure, though she thought the dark head turned back to look up at the windows.

Even if he did, he would probably not have seen her, Candy knew. Certainly he would not have been able to make out her frantic gesturing, she thought wryly. Especially as she was not sure what she was trying to convey—other than to stop him from going, of course.

In her ear, Judith had calmed a little.

'What am I going to *do*?' she was wailing.

Candy thought it was as much to herself as her daughter, but she answered anyway. It sounded harsh, but Candy had come to the end of the emotion she could spare on her mother's troubles.

'Get yourself a lawyer and change the locks.'

She put the phone down gently in the middle of Judith's exclamations.

* * *

It was not surprising, in the circumstances, she thought, that her mind was not wholly on the soup run that night. She had spent a fruitless evening trying to find Justin, and then a horrible half-hour trying to compose a note to him that explained, apologised, opened negotiations for the future, and all without hinting at the shameful truth.

Because there was no getting away from the fact that she was in love with him. Watching him drive away, Candy had felt a physical pain as if someone had plunged a hand into her breast and tried to haul the heart out of her. It had shocked her into gasping aloud. It was astonishing, she thought, that her mother had not heard it. But Judith was deaf to any troubles but her own, and the realisation was too new to Candy for her to tell anyone.

By the time she got to the Centre she was very nearly sure that she would never see him again. With a superstitious shiver, she remembered the advice she had given her mother. Maybe the next communication she had with Justin would be from a lawyer. Nobody noticed her distraction, though. They were all too busy.

'We're short-handed tonight,' Mel said over her shoulder. She was loading the catering packs of soup and coffee into the van. 'Dave's got an interview on *Eveningtime*. He forget to tell anyone.' She was carefully neutral.

Candy said abstractedly, 'The TV programme?'

Mel sent her a quick disbelieving look.

'Yeah,' she drawled, reaching for another substantial carton. 'Hand that up here.'

Candy complied mechanically.

'Were they the people here the day before yesterday?'

'Second cousins,' replied Mel cynically. 'Mr Tresilian is getting a lot of media attention this week.'

Candy shrugged, indifferent.

Mel paused in the loading and looked down at her out of the back of the van.

'You all right, Candy?'

Candy almost jumped. 'Of course,' she said in a strained voice. 'Why?'

Mel hesitated. 'You seem—a bit quiet.'

Candy shook her head. 'I've got things on my mind,' she said briefly. 'Nothing important. Let's get on with it.'

Mel looked sceptical. But she said nothing more. And there was certainly plenty to do.

Normally there were three of them on the van—one to drive and two to hand out the warm food. With Dave's unscheduled absence, there would only be two.

'I'll have to drive,' Mel told her worriedly. 'You're not licensed for this thing. But who'll stay and mind the shop?

'I don't think Candy ought to do it on her own,' said Robbie Mason firmly. 'Some odd characters wander in sometimes. It's no place for a girl on her own.'

'Nor's the van,' objected Mel. 'Some of the clients can be pretty weird too.'

Robbie looked perturbed. It was obvious he agreed with her. At last he said, 'It's safe enough with two of you as long as you don't leave the van.'

It sounded as if he was trying to convince himself.

Candy listened to the argument with blank indifference. All she could think of was the look of grim concentration on Justin's face as he drove off. He had looked as if he was going to the ends of the earth to get away from her.

Mel and Robbie settled it between them. Mel slammed shut the doors of the van and twisted the keys sharply in the lock. Then she pulled on her gloves and climbed up into the cab, holding the passenger door open for Candy.

'You *sure* you're all right?'

'Perfectly.'

'Not in any trouble?'

'No.'

Mel grimaced and turned on the ancient engine. 'Oh, well. Your funeral. You look pretty sick, though. Just throw up in the opposite direction, OK?'

Candy smiled faintly. 'I will.'

The engine was too noisy for them to talk much as they drove through the city. And when they stopped they were too busy. Candy was grateful for that. Mel was a shrewd observer.

As usual people were waiting for them: the old drunks, the young drop-outs, the disturbed, the lonely, the hurt. In handing out the warm soup and listening to their odd, dislocated conversation, Candy lost her sense of desolation for a while.

One of the more disturbed ones was upset, muttering to himself about thieves. Candy could not make it out.

'What's wrong with old Tozer?' she asked.

'Picked up his social security. Had it taken off him,' one of the others said. 'Them two kids. Cheek.'

And he jerked his head in the direction of the railway arches. The others nodded. They were sympathetic in their way, but they were used to unfairness.

Candy felt all the pain and frustrations of the last weeks build and concentrate. She looked at the bewildered old man, mumbling into his polystyrene cup, and was swept by a fury of indignation.

'Who are they?' she demanded.

They looked at her blankly.

'Couple of kids from the flats,' one volunteered. 'Seen them before. Not dossers.'

'Are they still there?'

'Suppose so,' they agreed. They were looking at each other uneasily.

Mel was preparing food behind her. She did not appear to have heard the conversation.

Candy said over her shoulder, 'You carry on here. There's something I want to sort out.'

'What?' Mel looked up from the soup she was stirring.

But Candy was already opening the doors of the van and swinging lightly down on to the pock-marked tarmac. Mel cried out in alarm. Candy ignored her.

The clients didn't like it. They had not seen anyone get out of the van before, and it unsettled them. One or two drew back in alarm.

Candy did not notice. Her eyes were set grimly on the shadowed arches. She ran down the cracked pavement. Her feet in their supple trainers made hardly any noise at all.

There was a light flickering deep in the recess of one of the arches. She could hear young voices laughing. She was so angry she could barely speak.

She ran lightly up to them and spun them round with a vicious pull on each shoulder. All her anger was in the movement.

'I suppose you think you've been very clever.'

The two faces that swung round were startled and very young. Why, they're hardly more than children, Candy thought, startled in her turn. Her anger began to die.

'Where is it?' she asked more gently. 'Old Tozer's money? What have you done with it?'

They looked scared.

'Nothing,' said one.

'It weren't us,' said the other. 'He took it. Freddy.' And he jerked his head to indicate the deeper arches.

The other one seemed to have recovered his bravado.

'Had it coming to him, Tozer, didn't he?' he said loudly. 'Silly old fool. Walking along the road, counting it like that. I could've told him. It were a temptation, weren't it? Not fair, holding out temptation.'

He sounded so sanctimonious that Candy could have hit him. Instead she gave him a look which made him step back involuntarily. Standing behind his friend's bony shoulder, he said in a quick high whine, 'Anyway, we ain't got it no more. Freddy took it off us when he saw we had it. Hit me, he did,' he added, with one wary eye on her reaction.

'You shouldn't have put temptation in his way, should you?' Candy said fiercely. 'You get me that money now, you nasty little thing.'

They both looked so terrified that it would have been comical in other circumstances. There were, after all, two of them, and she was a lightly built girl without weapons. But as she took a step forward the taller of them shot backwards, crying out, 'Freddy. Freddy.'

And a voice like a rattlesnake replied harshly out of the darkness, 'Yeah. I heard.'

Candy spun round. Not fast enough.

Before she knew what was happening, he had her in a street-fighter's grip, forcing her right arm cruelly high between her shoulder-blades. Her body arched and she gave a grunt of pain. Freddy enjoyed that. She heard it in the way he laughed.

'My word, it's Lady Bountiful,' he said in tones of mock gentility. 'What are you doing out of the charity wagon, darling? Looking for a bit of rough trade? You're not *really* interested in old Tozer, are you? Now the boys and me are more your age group.'

And he twisted her wrist so that she cried out.

'I can live with the dossers. They don't get in my way. But you bloody do-gooders. Sticking your noses in when they're not bloody wanted. This is my patch, darling. People do what I say here. And no slumming Sloane Ranger is going to muck that up. Understand?'

Behind them Candy could hear running feet. Voices. She did not know whether it was Freddy's reinforcements or someone that Mel had called up for help. They didn't have a phone in the van, so she'd have had to go looking for one. She'd have had too much sense to get out of the van and follow. Wouldn't she?

In Freddy's iron grip, Candy began to appreciate exactly how stupid she had been. She'd broken every rule they had: leaving the van, going into a dark place she didn't know, going on her own without proper care or support...

Freddy jerked her arm again. It was a vicious movement, but the limb was going numb. She registered the fact that he wanted to hurt, though.

'Understand?' he repeated in a snarl.

It occurred to Candy that if this episode got widely reported it would be very bad publicity for the homeless, and the Centre in particular. Conscience-stricken, she had a sudden vision of Dave Tresilian being asked to comment on the manhandling of one of his volunteers on his smart chat-show. He wouldn't be pleased.

In spite of the intolerable strain on her arm, she gave a little choke of laughter at the thought.

The sound had an electrifying effect on Freddy. He must have gone into shock. For a moment he almost let her go. Then he caught her back in a ferocious hold, forcing her head round to face him. His teeth showed.

'Laugh, will you? I'll teach you to laugh,' he said in a voice that sent a trickle of ice down Candy's spine.

His free hand flickered. She suddenly saw that he was holding a knife. The feeble firelight sparked along the slightly curved blade. She stared at it, mesmerised. This could not be happening. She did not believe it. All right, she had broken the rules, but real people did not behave like this.

The man called Freddy jerked his head at the smaller, meaner boy.

'Get out there and tell Love the World Incorporated that if they want their dossers' kitchen maid back it'll cost them,' he ordered. He grinned down at her, and the knife flashed as he flourished it. 'Not laughing now?' Over his shoulder he flung almost idly, 'Thousand quid, or I'll turn her into a jigsaw puzzle.'

Both boys gasped. For a moment Candy thought they were horrified by the violence of the threat. But she was soon disillusioned.

'Thousand quid?' The boy sounded as if he could not believe his ears. 'That lot haven't got a thousand quid. That old van of theirs is only good for scrap.'

'Then they'll have to raise it from their benefactors,' Freddy said in his mocking BBC announcer's voice. 'They'll find a way, won't they, doll?'

Staring up into his eyes, Candy realised suddenly that he hated her. He really hated her. She had invaded his territory, challenged his supremacy; and then she had laughed. He was not, she saw, going to let her go without hurting her. He owed it to himself.

She felt a surge of real terror. It must have shown in her body's involuntary reaction. Freddy smiled.

'Got a message for the world, doll?' he jeered softly. 'Mummy and Daddy? Boyfriend?'

Justin. Dear God, she would never see Justin again. And he was going to be so *hurt* after the way they had parted. Her eyes filled with irrepressible tears. Fortunately she did not think Freddy would be able to see them in the uncertain light. She turned her head away as far as she could.

'No.' It was a thread of a sound.

He shook her. 'What's that? I didn't hear you. Let's have that one again—with a laugh, as you're such a funny lady.'

Candy said nothing.

His grip hardened. 'You answer me when I'm talking to you. You hear me?'

But her head was swimming and her mouth felt full of cotton wool. She could not have answered him even if she wanted to.

Although he muttered impatiently, he seemed to sense it, because he jerked his head at the boy and said, 'Get going.'

The fuzziness in front of her eyes got worse. The flames of the tiny fire seemed to be leaping up to the ceiling and down, and there was a sound like a waterfall in her ears. She thought Freddy was shaking her, but she was not really sure.

Then suddenly he seemed to lose his temper and throw her into the fire. She screamed and put out her hands to save herself. But there was no fire. Only merciful blackness.

I'm fainting, thought Candy, astonished.

And knew no more.

CHAPTER NINE

CANDY was falling. It was the dream: her half-contrived fantasy of Dave playing St George to her manacled princess. Only this time, even in the dream, Candy knew it was for real. There was no hero to step out of the shadows and beat off her enemies. She had brought the thing about with her own silly fantasies and it served her right. This time she was on her own.

She tried to move. She was stiff and terribly cold. She was also afraid. If she moved *they* would see. And that would remind them, and they might... Even in the dream, her brain scuttled away from the thought of what *they* might do.

So she tried to move a tiny bit at a time, and found she could not. She was shaking convulsively. She could hear her own teeth chattering. But she could not move so much as her little finger.

Behind the rushing of the air and the skeletal rattling of her teeth there were other sounds. She stopped trying to move, and let her muscles go slack. The sounds came into focus.

They were voices. Angry voices, she thought, though they were not raised. Dave must be angry with her for her stupidity. She had got them into this.

'... reasonable offer,' a harsh, dry voice was saying.

She could not make out the reply. But there was something about the other voice that she recognised, like the note of a cello, deep and indistinguishable, but you knew it was there. It was a beautiful voice. But it had no place in the dream.

'Sure, you can try,' replied the harsh voice indifferently. 'But I know this place. You'll find her in the end. But by the time you do you might not want her.' His laugh was horrible.

She could hear steps, too. Someone was pacing on loose gravel or chippings. Not far away, but not immediately in front of her either. She thought they must be round a corner or behind a wall. She wished that her ears were not still ringing.

The second voice was clearer now.

'You'll have your money,' it said. It sounded calm.

'Oh, sure. With a police car waiting to give me a lift to the bank. Wake up.'

'I'm not leaving without her,' insisted the other voice.

'Nor am I. She may be your little helper, but she's my bloody life insurance. She stays with me.'

Candy frowned. Little helper? Did that mean Dave was there? But that wonderful deep brown voice wasn't Dave. If only she could *remember* ...

'No.' It was quite gentle but very firm.

'You're not listening to me.' The harsh voice was rising. He sounded as if he might be afraid.

'Yes, I am. But it's not going to do you any good, Armitage.'

'How do you know my name?' No doubt about the fear this time.

'Records. Files.' The voice was smooth as silk. 'You're a famous man in your way. You've been around longer than the dossers, they tell me.'

'You bloody soup-kitchen types. It's all a front. You're the fuzz. You're *spies*,' spat the harsh voice. The pacing footsteps grew faster and more uneven.

The voice was as calm as a millpond. 'I just want the girl. Nothing more. I'll even pay. But I won't go without her.'

Candy found she could turn her head. She did so. Her cheek was resting on dry earth that had a suffocating smell. Her whole skull throbbed.

'She's not here.' Harsh Voice was rattled. There was a panicky note in the ugly tones.

'Yes, she is.' The voice was gentle; you might have said it was amused but for that note of implacability. Candy was sure her captor could hear it too. 'You haven't moved and neither has she,' it said quietly.

'I have associates——' the other began to bluster.

But the voice was unimpressed. It cut in, 'When you've planned a job, no doubt you have. But this was pure opportunism, wasn't it, Armitage? You were out collecting your dues, and she came into your parlour; so you snapped her up. But you're still here. And so is she.'

There was a sudden stamping sound, as if the man who was pacing had stopped dead and swung round with a spurt of gravel.

'You think you're so clever.'

'No.' The other sounded terribly weary, Candy realised suddenly. 'No. But I can work out time as well as you. And I know what I have to do.'

'Citizen's arrest? A chap like you?' Harsh Voice sounded scornful. It had a genuine ring to it. 'Listen, the last time I was done, it took three of the pigs to take me in.'

'I don't want to take you in, Armitage. I want the girl.'

But the harsh-voiced man wasn't talking any more. Candy could hear in the voice and the careful steps that he was placing himself to spring. She tried desperately to wrench herself out of the dream, into the real world, to dispel the awful danger that she could smell all about her.

But she could not move. And then there was a thud, a cry of pain—quickly bitten off—running feet that came closer.

The sweat broke out on her forehead with the effort to wake up. And then she saw, like a sequence from a horror movie, a wildly wavering beam from a pencil torch and huge running shadows cast on lowering brickwork. She broke out of the dream and it was real.

They were shouting, both of them. It echoed round the cavernous interior of the old arches. Candy dragged herself up on her arms and looked wildly round. She was engulfed by the hideous shadow of two men fighting. They rolled and heaved and bit and punched like animals tearing a carcase. And, unmistakably, there was the gleam of torchlight on steel.

She cried out in horror.

For an instant the writhing shadow froze. Then it broke apart. It resolved itself into two crouching figures. They approached each other with horrible intent. Candy put the back of her hand to her mouth and forced back another cry. Her eyes smarted with effort, but she could not make out which was which.

She would not even know, she thought bitterly, when her hero lost.

There was a lunge, a sudden stab, then a brutally rapid overturning of the lunging figure. He went down with an unmistakable crack of bone.

Candy slumped against the wall. She could feel the brick through her thin T-shirt. It grazed her shoulderblades. She thought she had gone beyond fear, as the victor straightened and came heavily towards her.

The torch had gone out in the fight. But it made no difference. She knew she had brought this on herself. She had no hope of rescue.

He put his hand out to her, she thought, though it was difficult to tell in the dark. She could not see whether he still had the knife. She shrank away.

He said her name on a ragged breath. She did not recognise the voice and yet, somehow, everything that was in her opened and turned towards it.

And then, like the dream and yet not like the dream—because the fantasy hero used to swing her up in his arms, not stand in front of her with his chest heaving so that he could hardly get the words out—he said, 'Oh, my darling, I thought I'd lost you.'

She said in a disbelieving whisper, '*Dave*?'

He stopped dead.

And, half a second too late, Candy realised she had made a terrible mistake. She moved forward in protest. But the uneven ground began to shake beneath her feet and the air to rush past her again. She reached him and his arms closed round her. She could feel that his body was shaking. She was trembling too much herself to do anything but cling. She held him to her, incoherent—with remorse and relief and other more complicated emotions. He held her, stroking her hair with a hand that was still not steady. But he did not say anything more.

And eventually people came with lights. And a stretcher for the fallen, groaning body.

She tried to say something to him. But she could not form the words. And she was ashamed of the blatant need with which she clung on to him. There would never be any disguising that ever again.

He turned her in his arms. His hands were gentle. Impersonal. 'We must go. Can you walk?'

She stared up at him, mute. He touched her cheek, brushing away the dirt from where she had lain on the coal.

'Candida?'

Her eyes filled with tears. She dropped her head, burrowing it into his chest.

'Hold me,' she muttered, half not wanting to be heard, half begging.

He tensed as if she had touched a torn muscle.

He said sharply, 'Candida? Are you all right? Look at me.'

Behind them, another voice, kind and authoritative, said, 'Don't you worry, sir. She's had a nasty shock. Just a bit disorientated. She'll be OK after a cup of tea and a good cry.'

'Maybe.' He did not sound very sure.

He began to walk very gently back to the entrance of the arches, taking her with him. She leaned shamelessly against him, treasuring his strength. Once he dropped his head. She thought—imagined—he kissed her hair. She could have cried. She shrank closer to him.

There was an ambulance there, but they put her into the back of a police car. She held on to him, not wanting to be separated. But he detached her clutching hands.

He went down on his haunches beside the car. In the dark she could not read his expression, but his voice was kind. She hated the kindness. It hid the lack of love.

'Candida, you're all right now. Do you understand? It's Justin. You're safe.'

Someone brought her some tea in one of the van's polystyrene cups. Her hands were shaking too much, but Justin guided it to her lips. When she had hold of it his hands fell away.

Candy looked at him, stricken. How could she have called him Dave. *How*?

'What I said back there . . . I didn't realise . . .'

He gave her an odd lop-sided smile.

'Forget it.'

She gave him back the empty cup. He took it, looking down at it for a moment. Then he looked up at her with a curious smile.

'You've got a dirty face,' he said softly.

He reached in his pocket and offered her his handkerchief.

For some reason that hurt. It was as if symbolically he was telling her she was not his business. It was up to her to clean her own smudged face.

Candy shrank back. She knew her mouth was trembling, and despised herself for it.

Justin said her name in an urgent undertone. But it was too late. The others had come out of the arches, there were more police than she had ever seen before except when they were accompanying marches, and they were all getting into their cars and heading for the station.

Somebody said something to Justin. He rose to his feet.

'She's badly shaken. Can't it wait?'

'Just a brief statement tonight, sir. Then you can take your wife home.'

Home! Candy wondered desolately whether she still had any right to call Justin's flat home, and, if not, where he would send her. He would be kind, of course. The trouble was, kindness from him hurt like acid in an open wound. Not that he must ever know it.

She said, not realising she was saying it out loud, 'I have no home.'

'What?'

Justin bent down to her. But her head was dancing again, as the police cars switched on their headlights and their engines revved. Candy put a hand to her mouth.

'I feel sick,' she remarked conversationally.

And then, quite without warning, and for the second time in her life, fainted dead away.

She was never really sure what happened after that. There was a haze of light somewhere above her head. Out of the light there came voices—all angry this time.

'It's hopeless...'

'I must insist...'

'In this state, nothing she said would stand up in court anyway. Hasn't eaten all day, I'd say...'

'Hasn't *eaten*?'

'My client wishes...'

'Not yet...'

Then that deep, quiet voice that everyone listened to. 'Gentlemen, I am taking my wife home.'

It was all an extension of the dream. Except that for some reason she had stopped being afraid. Candy sank thankfully into exhausted sleep.

She woke slowly. The heaviness of sleep still clung around her as she opened her eyes and groaned.

Justin said impersonally, 'You'll feel better when you've eaten something.'

Candy lifted her head from the pillow, winced and let it drop back. She was in his room. She was alone in the big bed, the covers tangled and the pillows beaten flat. It could not have been more obvious that she had slept in it alone.

Justin was leaning against the wall by the window. His hands were in the pockets of his city trousers. He was wearing a crisp white shirt but no tie as yet. Presumably getting ready for the office.

'What time is it?'

Justin looked at his watch. 'Nearly eleven.'

She bounced up at that, though her every muscle screamed.

'*Eleven*? But—what are you doing here?'

He gave her a long, unreadable look.

'Waiting to see if you felt better,' he said evenly.

'Oh.' For some reason, Candy blushed. It was silly. There was no feeling in that cool voice. Certainly nothing to have her looking down at her interlocked fingers as if she were a Victorian maiden, and not managing to get her tongue round a reply. But she could feel the heat in her cheeks.

'Are you?'

She swallowed and fought for composure.

'Am I what?'

'Better,' he said patiently.

'Oh. Yes. I think so.'

He said very quietly, 'Don't lie to me, Candida. You look terrible.'

'Oh.' She cleared her throat. 'Er—maybe you're right. Breakfast could help.'

Justin looked at her searchingly. She could not meet his eyes. Which was stupid. He gave a sigh.

'I'll put the coffee on. And toast. An egg?'

Candy shuddered. Looking at him shyly under her eyelids, she saw him frown.

'They said at the hospital you hadn't eaten all day yesterday.' It was an accusation. 'Why, for God's sake?'

Yesterday was a century ago. Candy struggled to remember what happened. The fight with Justin. And her mother. And her own wretched bewilderment. And then Lizbeth, in tears at her meeting with Justin, presenting a challenge Candy could not begin to meet. The slowly dawning realisation that she had locked herself into a prison she would never get out of by falling in love with Justin.

She winced. And because she could not bear to think about it, she took refuge, as she always did, in comedy. She shrugged.

'Oh—unrequited love.'

It was even true, she thought drily.

Justin's face darkened. He took a hasty step forward. Then stopped.

'One day...' he said, the beautiful mouth rigid.

Candy tossed back her hair. She realised, startled, that her shoulders were bare. 'Yes?' she asked defiantly.

'Oh, God, you're such a *child*!' Justin exploded. 'You play with fire and don't even... One day you'll get yourself badly burned.'

She stared at him. For once his face was not expressionless. The rage was there for anyone to see. She said involuntarily, 'I think I already did.'

The anger died out of his eyes. For a moment he didn't speak, the keen eyes searching her face.

Then he said, 'Poor little Candy.'

He had never used that tone to her before. It hit her like a blow. It was as if he had removed himself. As if they were strangers.

Candy sat up straighter, but he had turned away.

'I'll bring you a tray.'

'No,' she said more sharply than she intended.

It was odd, but she knew she could not bear that— the illusion of being cherished when he was just being courteous. Courteous, responsible Justin, who regarded his marriage as a terrible mistake.

He turned back, mildly surprised.

She said hurriedly, 'I want to get up. I'd like a shower. I feel sweaty and yuck.' One eyebrow rose disbelievingly as she snapped, 'You said yourself I looked terrible.'

Justin looked amused. 'Not too terrible to have breakfast in bed.'

But she was obstinate. He shrugged.

'Don't be long, then. Or I'll come and get you.'

It was not, she knew, an idle threat. But it was a wholly disinterested one. Responsible Justin making sure that his nuisance of a wife didn't faint in the shower. She could have thrown things.

Instead she waited until he had gone and then slipped out of bed. Whoever had undressed her last night had failed to find a nightdress. She was naked. Candy bit her lip.

There was no point in thinking about it now. It would have to have been Justin. And, after all, he had seen her naked before. There was no reason why it should make her feel so shaky and vulnerable to realise he had stripped off yesterday's blackened garments.

She set her teeth and grabbed at the old robe on the chair at the end of the bed. It was rubbed thin with wear and the cuffs were fraying. It smelled of Justin's cologne.

A lump came into her throat. She swallowed hard and went to her own room to collect jeans and a shirt. But she went back to Justin's bathroom to shower.

He did not disturb her. She was very quick and he would have had no justification. But Candy had half hoped that he might come back into the room to tell her that coffee was brewed or the toast nearly ready, as he had done in the cottage.

Suppressing disappointment, she ran a comb perfunctorily through her curls and went out to the kitchen.

There was another disappointment. Jeremy was there, looking interested and sipping mango tea. Justin gave them a smile of equal impersonal friendliness and put toast and a boiled egg in front of Candy.

Since she had seen him earlier he had put on his waistcoat and tie. So he had to have come back into the bedroom, and had not called out to her. And he was going into the office after all.

'Thank you,' she said in a constricted voice, sitting down at the pine table.

He looked at his watch. 'You'll be all right now.' It wasn't a question.

Candy wanted to reach out and beg him to stay. She wanted to say that she had not really thought he was

Dave last night. That it was a spur-of-the-moment confusion, coming from her own silly fantasies. That she had not *wanted* Dave. That she wanted nobody but Justin and she wanted him forever.

It was impossible. Jeremy was there; and anyway, it would embarrass Justin horribly. He had already been more than dutiful.

He bent and kissed her cheek. His lips just brushed the softness beside her mouth, but her whole body clenched in response. Unseen, her hands shut tight in her lap as she fought down the urge to lock them behind his head and make him kiss her properly. As he could.

He caught up his jacket from a chair-back, picked up his briefcase, said goodbye to Jeremy—and went.

She could not help it. Candy watched him all the way to the door with her heart in her eyes. He did not turn. The door closed behind him; he ran lightly down the stairs; the front door on to the street slammed. It had a final sound.

Jeremy was watching her. She realised with a little start that his shrewd eyes had been on her throughout. He shook his head and brought his tea over to the table. He pulled up the chair that Justin had pushed awry when he'd seized his jacket. Lifting his cup, Jeremy looked at her gravely over the rim.

'Now, dear,' he said seriously. 'I think you'd better tell me all about it.'

When she had finished, Candy could not meet his eyes. Jeremy was looking at her incredulously. Candy bent her head.

'I have never,' said Jeremy, 'heard such rubbish in my life. For heaven's sake, I thought you were a sensible girl. That's what Justin said. How wrong can you be?'

Candy bit her lip. 'When did he say it?'

'When he told me you were getting married. After he'd been to some party of your father's.'

She stared. 'You must be mistaken.'

Jeremy shook his head positively. 'No, I'm not. He had his aunt Rose round here for breakfast. They were into the sausages and bacon by the time I arrived. And they'd opened champagne. Lady Richmond said, "Justin's getting married at last. Be gentle with him, Jeremy, he's in love." And Justin grinned and gave me a glass of champagne.'

Candy said, 'I don't believe it.'

He shrugged. 'Believe it or not, it's the truth. Ask Lady Richmond.'

'But—we'd only just met,' she said blankly.

Jeremy looked faintly interested. 'Love at first sight?'

'Don't be ridiculous,' exclaimed Candy. She stood up, agitated. 'That's just in fairy-stories. Love at first sight! Anyway, people don't get *married* because of it. They get married for reasons—after thinking things over and...and...'

She stopped under Jeremy's amused eyes.

'And what were Justin's reasons?' he asked politely.

She flung up her hands, helpless. 'How do I know? He's not the sort of man who would *say*. I thought maybe the shares in the company that were in trust for me...' She trailed off, meeting Jeremy's sceptical look.

'He must have said something,' he said briskly. 'Think. When he asked you——'

'Told me,' she interjected.

'All right. Told you. He must have said there was something in it for both of you. What was it?'

She thought. Then she said slowly, 'He said that I needed a Galahad.'

'Well, he wasn't wrong, was he?' Jeremy remarked not without sympathy.

'Of course not. I'm perfectly capable of looking after myself without some knight in shining armour——'

'You,' interrupted Jeremy calmly, 'were so scared when he walked out of here this morning, I thought you were going to collapse all over again.'

'Oh,' said Candy.

'Weren't you?'

'I was shaken after last night. I——'

Jeremy looked disgusted. He got up, pushing the chair away decisively.

'If you want my advice you'll take a long, hard look at yourself before you do some serious damage,' he said. 'Not that it's any of my business. I must get on with my work.'

He buzzed angrily round the flat with his Hoover. Candy followed him, but he kept shaking his head, insisting that he couldn't hear. 'Anyway, it's not me you need to talk to. It's Justin. After the police, of course. You do know they're coming this morning?'

She looked blank. He clicked his tongue.

'Justin talked them out of it last night. But they want a statement.'

'Why didn't Justin tell me?'

Jeremy sniffed. 'Seems you two aren't communicating these days. It's up on the kitchen memo-board. *I* saw it first thing. Perhaps you didn't look.'

There were two policemen—one big and slow and quite young, the other older and obviously considerably his senior.

'Thank you, Mrs Richmond,' he said when they had finished. 'I wasn't best pleased with you last night, I don't mind admitting. Or your husband, for that matter. Armitage is dangerous—a professional with a mad streak. Mr Richmond had no cause to go in after him like that. And if that old tramp hadn't called we wouldn't have known what was going on.' He stood up. 'Still, no harm done, seeing as you're all right. And Mr Richmond too, I hope?'

Candy looked blank.

The younger policeman stood up too. He commented, 'That was a nasty cut on his hand. And a lot of blood, too, if that really was all that was wrong with him. He wouldn't let the police surgeon look at him last night. Too worried about you.'

He didn't actually say he couldn't understand it. He didn't have to. The older policeman looked amused.

'You wait till you're married, Geoff. You'll know what it's like then,' he said cheerfully. Geoff looked sceptical. His senior said soberly, 'It wasn't just you had a shock last night, Mrs Richmond. I'd say your husband's going to get a nasty reaction, if he isn't careful. He was going crazy before he went in there after Armitage. Gave my men the slip doing it. I reckon that'll take some getting over.'

Candy stood up too. Justin had been *hurt* last night?

'Yes,' she said. 'I mean, thank you.'

Something about her blank look must have touched the older policeman. He gave her an almost fatherly pat on the arm.

'You take care of him. And yourself. Get away. A good holiday does wonders. Make a bit of a fuss of yourselves.'

'Yes,' she said again.

Unbidden the thought of the French cottage came into her mind. It would be high summer now—hot and sleepy amid the vines. Justin loved it, and together they could start to talk again. Maybe even touch a little.

She gave them a sudden, brilliant smile. 'I'll think about it,' she promised.

When she had showed them out, Jeremy came out of the kitchen with his tote bag.

'Your mother rang,' he said, consulting a list. 'And some woman from the Centre—Mel, is it? And the bloke who runs it. And Alison. She said the papers had picked it up, and Justin's referring them all to his Press officers.'

Candy waited. When he was clearly not going to say anything else, she could not help herself.

'Not Justin?'

Jeremy said drily, 'You want to talk to Justin, you call him.'

She sighed. It wasn't so easy to call someone you saw night and morning and weren't sure wanted to hear any more from you.

Jeremy slapped the list down on the telephone table.

'Up to you, Candy. There's your messages. See you.'

He went. She sat for a long time trying to make up her mind. At the very thought of speaking to him, her hands shook. This is crazy, she thought. I married the man, for heaven's sake. I can't be afraid of him. She took four long breaths, picked up the phone and rang the private office number.

Alison answered, sounding friendlier than she had for weeks. Justin was busy, but she would just see whether he could take a call. And she did hope Candy was better after her ordeal.

'Thank you,' said Candy, surprised and touched.

'I do so admire you for doing it. And so does Justin, I know. If he seems a bit short-tempered about it, that's because he worries about you.'

That was the third person this morning telling her that Justin cared for her. Could they all be wrong? But if they weren't, how had she managed to be so blind?

'Candida.' It was Justin's voice, low and resonant and infinitely attractive. Candy felt her heart begin to beat faster.

'Hello,' she said, like a breathless schoolgirl.

'Are you all right?' he asked with quick concern.

'Oh, yes. I—I've just seen the police. They—they told me you were hurt last night.'

There was a little pause. Then he said oddly, 'Is that why you rang?'

She didn't know what to say. If only he were *here* and she could look at him and touch him and he could see what she felt. She had no idea how to put her uncertainties, her need for reassurance into words.

'Yes. No. Sort of.'

'Don't start feeling sorry for me, Candida.' The velvet voice was harsher than she would have believed possible. 'I'm not one of your lame dogs. I don't need your pity.'

So much for her fantasy of them together in the French countryside refashioning the future.

Candy said, 'I was worried.'

She knew she sounded sullen, and was furious with herself.

Justin told her drily, 'I'll survive. Now, did you want something else, or can we leave the rest of this domestic exchange until I get home this evening?'

Suddenly Candy was angry. She had sunk her pride to telephone him, and he was just scoring points off her.

'We can leave it forever, as far as I'm concerned,' she snapped, and slammed the phone down.

After that she went through the other messages like a rotor mower. She told Mel that she was fine, Dave that she did not want to join him in a Press conference, and her mother that she would not get involved any more in her marital squabbles.

'*What*?' Judith sounded blank.

'I'm sorry, Mother,' said Candy with unprecedented briskness, 'but it's not my problem. You married him. You sort it out. Or leave him. But don't keep calling me in to referee. It's not fair, and it gets you nowhere.'

'*Candy*!' exclaimed her mother, shocked.

'I've been your champion for too long, Mother,' Candy went on. 'You need to stand up to him yourself. No one else can do it for you.'

'But he's so impatient with me,' wailed Judith.

'Mother,' said Candy with patience, 'if you don't start standing up for yourself, he won't be the only one.'

'I'll come over for coffee,' Judith said. 'I was going to Harrods——'

'No,' Candy interrupted firmly. 'I've got problems of my own. I need a bit of space for a while.'

'But——'

'*Please*, Mother.'

'You're abandoning me.' Judith's voice rose to the point of sub-hysteria, which usually had Candy backing down.

She thought of Justin's cold voice on the telephone and the warmth of his arms when he had caught her last night; which was real? She had to find out. For once her mother's dramas left her unmoved.

'No, I'm not,' she denied gently. 'But I need to sort out my own life for a bit. Not yours. Good luck, Mother. Call me in a month or so.'

And she put the phone down on disbelieving silence.

She made herself some of Jeremy's mango tea, and sat in the window seat with it. Below her the traffic roared silently, a tribute to the excellent window insulation. She looked round the flat.

It was still Justin's. Even after Jeremy's encouragement, she had not tried to change anything. Even her books were stored neatly in her own room. She had not bought a rug or a picture or a record. She had not even bought the clothes he wanted her to have.

What was it that he had said all those weeks ago? That being married should be fun? Fun! She had been proud and prickly, looking for signs that he didn't want her.

But in France, when they had walked and shopped and read together, it had not seemed that he didn't want her. In fact he had seemed as surprised by that sudden flowering of friendship as she was.

What if he wasn't a calculating Titan like her father? What if he was just another bewildered creature like herself, surrounded by family he didn't understand and wasn't really part of? Doing things because he was good at them rather than because he enjoyed them? Just like her?

He enjoys playing the violin, she thought. And walking in the country. And he enjoyed making love to me.

The memory set a little flicker alight inside her.

She made a decision.

It was late in the afternoon when she got to the Centre. For once she had brought her car. Daytime parking was problematical, but it would be easier to get home, and problems, she told herself firmly, were meant to be solved.

She was going through the schedule with Mel, shifting duties for the coming weeks, when Dave walked in. He swept her up in a bear-hug. She blinked at him, fending him off.

'Candy, my angel, I knew you wouldn't let us down. The TV crew will be here at six and——'

'Shut up, Dave,' said the newly confident Candy without rancour.

He was so astonished that he did. Mel hid a smile.

'I'm not parading before any damned cameras. You can forget it. I've just come to sort out a break for a bit,' she told him.

He could understand that. He told her so with a forgiving smile. He said they should go into his office and he would explain to her what it was that she *really* wanted to do.

'What I really want to do,' Candy assured him, 'is spit in your eye.'

He was dumbfounded. But he recovered himself. She was in shock. She didn't mean it.

'I mean it, Dave,' she said grimly. 'I've had just about enough of being told what I really am and what I really want by you. You're so damned clever at running other people's lives that you never notice what a hash you're making of your own. What are you going to do when the media get tired of you? It's going to be awfully boring back there on the beat with the van.'

He was wounded. But there was the beginning of anger there too. Mel got up, murmuring an excuse, and went out. Dave ignored her.

When she had gone, Candy said, 'You like an audience, Dave. The volunteers. The TV people. Whoever. Me. You had me on a string for years, and you enjoyed it. A few confidences, a few hugs and I fell, didn't I? And that was just what you wanted.'

'No,' he said in a strangled voice.

'And then I got married and you thought, That's all right, it's only a social thing. She's still my property emotionally.' She was so angry, her voice choked. 'Only you were wrong, and you didn't like it. So you decided to pull me back on the roadshow with a slightly hotted-up version.'

Dave stood up. He looked angry. He shouted, 'No. I *love* you.'

Behind them the old ill-fitting door that had been closed slammed back. They spun round. Neither had heard the man enter.

Justin surveyed them quietly.

Candy's heart sank to her toes. He couldn't have come in at a more incriminating moment. And—remembering their last telephone conversation—what was he doing here, when he ought to have been at work sorting out important, undomestic problems?

She glared at him. His lips twitched and one eyebrow rose. But he gave no other sign of reaction.

Dave stepped forward as if to protect her, his best profile in relief, his chin high. Justin looked at them both with that damned unreadable expression that made her want to throw things.

'Well? he prompted gently. 'That was a declaration, my dear. You have to answer; it's only polite.'

Dave was so startled that he dropped his chin and stopped looking noble.

'It was not,' retorted Candy with precision, 'a declaration. It was Dave's way of keeping up the groupie quota.' She tuned to face him, and saw with satisfaction that for once he seemed utterly at a loss. 'Listen to me, Dave. I do this because I think it's important. And on the whole I do it well. Last night was stupid and I'm ashamed.'

Dave started to speak. She held up her hand.

'*Ashamed*, Dave. I don't want to go playing heroines with the Press. I've had that sort of silliness knocked out of me. I put a lot of people at risk last night. I was frightened half out of my wits. And——' she gagged a bit but went on bravely'—my husband was hurt. All because of me. I want to put it behind me and do better in the future.'

'Eventually,' murmured Justin.

Candy was startled. She turned her head. 'What?'

'Eventually. When you come back,' he said softly.

Dave's eyes narrowed. 'Are you forbidding her to come here?'

'For a while,' Justin confirmed with composure.

The last of Dave's nobility dropped from him. Chin jutting, he looked like a thug.

'You think Candy'll just do what you say?'

Justin's face took on that inner amusement she knew so well.

'I very much doubt it.'

'Well, then . . .'

'So I'm going to kidnap her,' Justin said calmly. 'Now.'

Dave put both arms round her shoulders and pulled Candy into the shelter of his body.

'You'll deal with me first,' he asserted, noble again.

Justin sighed. 'No doubt that could be arranged. But really I've had enough fighting for this quarter. And we'd do an awful lot of damage in here,' he added, looking round the small office.

This practical reflection took the steam out of Dave's heroics a bit. Candy detached herself carefully. Justin nodded with approval.

'Coming, then, Candida?'

Her eyes narrowed. 'Not because you say so,' she said belligerently.

'Naturally not.'

She turned back to Dave. 'I'll be back. I've talked to Mel. But I don't want any of your nasty, manipulative little games any more. When I come back it will be on a strictly professional basis.'

Dave protested, 'Candy, you can't do this to me.'

Her spine went rigid.

Justin said softly, 'You had your chance, Tresilian. Better listen to the lady.'

'Goodbye, Dave,' Candy said, head high.

She walked out of the office just ahead of Justin. Four months ago, she could never have imagined leaving Dave like this. Justin took her elbow.

'Where's your car?'

She looked at him in surprise, blinking away the film in front of her eyes.

'Over there. Why?'

'I took a cab.' He looked down at her. 'Would you like me to drive?'

She bristled at once. 'Why?'

He put an infinitely gentle forefinger to her damp
lashes and lifted off a dew-drop.

'Crying and driving. Not illegal. But not recom-
mended, I believe.'

She stared at him for a long moment. He was grave
and kind but there was no fire there. She said it to herself
deliberately: no love. He opened the passenger door for
her, and closed it on her courteously before going round
to the driver's side and seating himself behind the wheel.
The tears spilled over.

'Damn you, Justin,' she said.

CHAPTER TEN

JUST for a moment Candy had a fine sense of achievement. She could sense the astonishment in the silence behind her in the Centre. Astonishment and, she thought, reluctant admiration. She felt rather proud of herself, at least as long as she did not think about Justin or the reasons for his unexpected arrival.

Without another word, he started the engine. She looked at him under her lashes. As usual, his expression told her nothing. As usual, he did not speak. Candy suddenly realised that he looked paler than normal.

She said involuntarily, 'Are you all right?'

Justin was looking straight ahead at the incoming traffic. His mouth quirked wryly.

'You mean after going three rounds with the Viking? Metaphorically speaking, of course.'

Candy flushed. 'I meant after last night,' she said stiffly. She remembered suddenly that the policemen had said that Justin had been covered in blood. She studied his profile anxiously.

Justin said suddenly, 'You don't think I have any right to care about you, do you, Candy?'

She was astonished. 'I don't know what you mean.'

Justin gave a harsh laugh. 'Well, you didn't expect me to come after you yesterday, did you? You were frightened and in danger, but you didn't think I would be there for you.' He sent her a rapid unsmiling look before turning the car on to a main road. 'You expected the Viking.'

169

She flinched. There was a long pause. Oh, God, this was awful. Of course he would think that. She had called him Dave. She could have cut out her tongue. She twisted her hands hopelessly.

Then he asked softly, 'Was that who you really wanted, Candy?'

'No.' It was no more than a breath, though she would have liked to shout it from the house-tops.

There was nothing in Justin's expression to show that he had even heard. He put the car round a corner with precision. Candy suddenly noticed that they were pulling on to a motorway. She turned, startled. It had never occurred to her that they were not going back to the flat.

'Where are you taking me?'

Justin laughed. 'Neutral territory.'

Candy stared at him. He looked implacably ahead. Although she was certain from the set of his head that he was aware of her astonishment.

'You mean you really are kidnapping me?'

He nodded.

'Where?'

Justin shrugged. 'Halloways.'

Candy stared harder. 'Halloways? You mean the Richmond family place? But——'

'But it's a bloody great castle,' Justin agreed grimly. 'I know. I pay a lot of the bills. It wouldn't be my hide-away, but I rather doubt whether you have your passport on you.'

Candy remembered how she, too, had thought of returning to the cottage in France. She gave a little choke of laughter. Justin went on as if he hadn't heard.

'No one will be there mid-week. I rang and made sure. Anyway, the western tower is mine, and people know they're not allowed there without invitation. We won't be disturbed.'

Candy said softly, 'Why?'

Justin gave her a swift look. 'I don't encourage my family to invade my privacy.' A slight flush stole into his pale cheeks. 'Our privacy.'

'That wasn't quite what I meant,' Candy said carefully. 'I meant why do we need to be undisturbed?'

Justin's mouth tightened, but he said, drawling more than usual, 'I would think that is self-evident.'

Candy deliberately relaxed her limbs. She could feel the tension in the back of her neck running all the way down to the ends of her fingers. She looked steadily ahead out of the windscreen at the ribbon of brilliant road that streamed towards them. Justin was driving fast. She looked at the long-fingered, capable hands on the wheel and gave a long, luxurious shiver.

But all she said was, 'Not to me.'

Justin replied evenly, 'I can't drive and bare my soul at the same time. If you want a fight it'll have to wait.'

Candy shivered again. Looking at him under her lashes, she said, 'I wasn't thinking of fighting.'

Justin gave a harsh laugh. 'Well, that will be a pleasant change, at least.'

The house, when they arrived, was everything that Candy expected: formal gardens, long, sweeping drive between beech trees, and turreted edifice. She was too intent on the man beside her to be intimidated by the formal elegance, however.

Justin swept round the corner of the drive and into what appeared to be a disused stable. There were other vehicles there, but nobody in evidence. He slid her car neatly into a stall beside a 1930 coupé and killed the engine.

'Come on.'

Candy followed him out of the stable yard and round a high grey stone wall. Eventually they came to a small wooden door. Justin opened it, bracing his arm against it to allow her to pass through. On the other side was an aspect of lawns and summer flowers like a secret garden out of a dream. Her lips parted in amazement. She stopped.

Justin was selecting another key that Candy had never seen before. He went to a massive oak door in a rounded turret that looked like something out of the *Tales of Camelot*. Candy watched, fascinated. She fully expected the ancient thing to open with a creak of unoiled hinges. But in fact it swung wide as easily as their own front door in the flat.

Turning, Justin held out an imperative hand. Candy went to him.

Inside it struck dim. Candy gave a little shiver at the shadowed sunlight. Immediately Justin's arm went went round her. He guided her into a comfortable sitting-room with leaded windows from floor to ceiling, admitting the sunlight on to large, shabby sofas and armchairs.

He pulled her down on to the sofa in front of the unlit fireplace and turned her towards him. His face was unreadable.

'And now...'

His mouth was not unreadable at all. The hunger was naked. When she could speak, Candy said, 'Why...?'

Justin drew back. In the dim light the planes and angles of his face were all shadow.

'I know you didn't want to marry me. You never made any bones about it. In fact——' he looked at her searchingly '—I always thought that if your mother hadn't got herself into that mess over her gambling you wouldn't have considered it for a moment.'

Candy looked down at their clasped hands. It was probably true. Conscience flicked its whip at her. She withdrew her hand from his. Justin made no attempt to recapture it.

'But you said—if you remember—there were no lovers. No one else.'

Candy caught her breath, looking up quickly. 'That was important?'

Justin looked at her. He was very grave.

'The most important thing in the world.' He gave a short laugh. 'Only you have your own way of telling the truth. It wasn't until afterwards that I realised——'

'What?'

He looked at her steadily. 'That you had been frightened. By someone you liked. Perhaps loved.'

She made an involuntary movement, quickly curbed.

'Will you tell me the real truth now, please, Candy? Was it David Tresilian?' His voice hardened. 'And are you going to stay in love with him forever?'

Candy made a strangled sound. No words came.

Justin sighed. 'I thought it was going to be so easy. I knew you were very innocent. But I had enough experience for both of us, I thought. And I knew the prison you were in with your parents. I'd been there myself. I could understand that you wanted to run away from all that. Well, I would help you.' He paused. 'What I hadn't allowed for was that you were running away from David Tresilian as well.' His mouth twisted. 'From unrequited love, in fact.'

Candy's flush deepened. Her girlish dreams hadn't amounted to love. She knew that now. She felt embarrassed at her stupidity.

And Dave wasn't the hero she'd made of him. He was a good, kind man with a driving enthusiasm and as much sensibility as a wart-hog. Whereas Justin knew things he hadn't told him, because he listened, listened properly, not just to the words. And fastidious, private Justin had squared up to a thug for her, gone out into a dangerous, violent world and bargained with a criminal—and he thought he hadn't any right to care about her.

Tears almost clogged her throat. 'I didn't know——' she began.

He made a small, fierce movement, quickly stilled. She broke off, flinching.

But all he said was, 'Yes, I think we were both taking a bigger gamble than we realised.'

He got up. The late afternoon sunlight caught the reddish lights in his dark hair and made it gleam like polished wood. Candy caught her breath momentarily at the sheer beauty of it. He thrust his hands into his pockets. With his back to her he stood looking out through the long, leaded panes across the riot of summer flowers to the hazy hills beyond.

'So what do we do now?'

Candy stared at the set of the broad shoulders outlined against the window.

'I don't understand,' she said in a voice that shook slightly.

'No?' Justin sounded tired. He shrugged. 'Well, we'd better make up our minds whether the gamble has come off or not. You haven't been happy, I think. Last night——' He gave a sharp sigh. 'Things haven't worked out as I'd intended.' He shrugged again, turning back to face her. 'In any way.'

Candy said slowly. 'What happened last night, Justin? What did I do to make you——?' She broke off with a helpless gesture.

He said wearily, 'You didn't do anything. I just realised how far apart we were still. Married three months and you looked at me as if I were a stranger.'

'Oh, God,' Candy said under her breath.

She wanted to put her arms round him, but she didn't quite dare. He looked very remote and unapproachable silhouetted against the ancient window.

'I'm not good at close relationships. I'm not used to them. I haven't lived with a woman since the divorce.'

He gave a laugh that held no amusement. 'In fact that was one of the things Marianne complained about—that I wasn't prepared to give enough time to the relationship, even then——' He broke off.

He looked very isolated. Candy couldn't help herself. She went to him in pure instinct and put her arms round him. His arms closed round her, but absently. It was not much more than a courtesy. He was obviously lost in his memories.

'This time was going to be different,' he said over her head. 'I was determined. I took you off to France where no one could find us or get in the way, and—it was a disaster.'

Candy flinched. Justin looked down at her quickly.

'Oh, it wasn't your fault,' he told her in a gentle voice. 'You'd been quite straight with me. You'd certainly never given me any reason to imagine that you wanted anything more than you'd contracted for. The trouble is, I'd forgotten how young you were. You said you didn't want a cheating marriage, but every time I touched you, you seemed horrified.'

Candy said, 'No,' in an appalled undertone, but Justin did not appear to hear her.

'The crazy thing is that I knew. Underneath, I knew I was too old for you. But I've always been a gambler. And if it came off it was going to be the whole world.'

Hadn't he said something of the kind to her once? 'The longer the odds, the greater the rewards'? Something like that.

'I'd never known a girl who muddled hero worship and love, and then went and gave her silly heart on the strength of it.'

There was pain in the even tones. Candy felt like crying. She had never felt so out of her depth before. She hugged him, but she did not know what to say.

'And then—that night when you came back and he was with you—I saw you. Did you know that? I—needed to talk and I never seemed to be able to get you to spend time with me. So I was looking out for you, and when I saw your car I came down.'

Candy caught her breath.

'You saw Dave kiss me?' she said in a strangled whisper.

Justin held her away from him and looked down into her face.

'I saw you kissing,' he agreed ironically. 'I wouldn't have said you were struggling.'

Candy was tense and bewildered, strung between hope and a terror that he wanted the marriage ended forever. But this she could deal with.

She said crisply, 'He jumped on me without warning. I think I'd stopped being as adoring as he likes his helpers to be, so he was bringing me back into line. I told him I didn't appreciate it. He was very offended. Didn't you see him stalk off to the bus stop?'

Justin's eyes narrowed. He shook his head. 'I backed away as fast as I could. I didn't want you to think I'd been spying on you. I wasn't going to mention it. But when you came in, looking so *alive*, I just lashed out.' A faint flush came into the tanned cheeks. 'I've never forgiven myself for that.'

'For making love to me?' Candy asked with a very fair appearance of coolness, though her heart was thumping uncomfortably.

Justin's eyes glinted at that.

'I can't honestly say that, no. But for using that experience of mine to persuade you into something I knew you didn't want.'

Candy swallowed. But she met his eyes bravely.

'It seemed to you I didn't want it?' she asked politely.

He laughed, but his eyes were sad. 'Not at the time, no. But you were off balance, and it was all new to you. And sexual attraction is a powerful editor of the emotions. You couldn't be expected to know that. But I could. I did. And you realised it soon enough in the morning.' His face was bleak suddenly. 'You couldn't bear the sight of me.'

Candy removed herself from his arms. She put her hands behind her back and lifted her chin.

'I was embarrassed,' she said clearly. 'And it seemed as if *you* couldn't bear the sight of *me*.'

Justin stared at her. She could feel the hot colour surging into her face, and resolutely ignored it. But his fascinated inspection didn't help.

'Embarrassed?' he echoed faintly.

Candy glared at him. 'It's all very well for you. As you've pointed out, you've got decades of experience to draw on.'

'Not *decades*,' Justin protested.

Candy swept on, ignoring the mischievous murmur, 'I'd never done anything like that before, and I—didn't know I could go out of control like that. I thought——'

Justin seemed to have regained his habitual calm amusement, she saw with dudgeon. One black eyebrow rose. She blushed furiously.

'Well, if you must know, I thought it as a bit excessive. And I thought you might find it—oh, I don't know, embarrassing. Even disgusting.'

The amusement disappeared as if she had blasted it out of him with a machine gun. He looked horrified.

'*What*?'

'Bear in mind it was all new to me.' Candy reminded him of his own words, not without a certain satisfaction. 'And you'd not shown any signs of wanting to be with me since we came back from France. I thought if I dumped my adolescent lusts—to say nothing of my heart—at your feet, you'd hate it.'

He took a hasty step forward.

'*What* did you say?'

She glared at him. 'You heard perfectly well.'

Justin shook his head. 'Yes, but I didn't believe it,' he said candidly. 'You've been running for all you're worth ever since France. Even before.'

Candy shook the hair out of her eyes, leaned forward and hissed, 'Because I didn't know how you felt. You said we could have fun being married. *Fun*,' she emphasised grimly, 'not high romance and undying devotion. What was I supposed to do? Say, "I'm awfully sorry but I think I may be falling in love with you, after all"? You didn't talk to me, take any interest in anything I did——' She broke off with an angry sob.

Justin sat down slowly on the window seat. He held out his hand to her. Candy shook her head.

'Come here,' he said levelly. 'Please.'

She swallowed and protested hardly, 'Justin, I still don't know what you feel.'

He gave her an incredulous look. 'I would've thought I'd made it obvious enough.'

Candy set her teeth. 'Not to me.'

He smiled. 'Then come and sit here and let me explain.' She hesitated, and his smile grew. 'Or are you afraid?'

At once she went and sat next to him on the window seat, not touching or appearing to notice the hand that was still extended. He gave a little nod, and half turned on the chintz cushions to face her. But he did not attempt again to touch her. He said quietly, 'When we met I wasn't looking for a wife. Or a girlfriend,' he added quickly at her cynical look. 'I'd been there, done that, and frankly I didn't want to get into that sort of mess again.'

Candy listened, head bent. She deliberately avoided looking at him. She had come to recognise every nuance in the smooth voice, but that handsome, guarded face could deceive her all too easily. Though now, she thought, he was telling the truth.

'Then why did you ask me to marry you?' she asked bluntly.

Justin leaned back into the oak corner. He seemed very relaxed, but she could sense the tension in the lounging body. She knew he was watching her, but she still refused to look up.

'Now there you have one of life's great mysteries,' he drawled. 'It didn't fit in at all well with my plans. In fact it didn't fit in with anybody's plans.' He paused. 'Including yours, my darling,' he said deliberately.

She did look up then, flushing quickly at the endearment. The warmth in his eyes made her look away; her heart leaped too crazily at it.

She said gruffly, 'Or Lizbeth Lamont's.'

Justin looked taken aback.

'Lizbeth?'

'She more or less told me she was an old flame. And that I wasn't much of a rival,' Candy reminded him with rancour.

His eyes glinted. 'I remember. It was one of the few times that gave me hope.'

Her brow creased. 'Because she was jealous? But why on earth didn't you ditch me and marry her? Or live with her or whatever you wanted?' she demanded impatiently.

Justin sighed with impatience. 'It gave me hope,' he said carefully, 'because *you* were jealous. I don't give a damn about Lizbeth Lamont, and never did. It's mutual—and we both know it.'

Candy wanted desperately to believe him. But Jeremy had said they had been lovers, and Jeremy was no mischief-maker. And that conversation she had so reluctantly overheard was not easy to forget. The way her mother had swept her off, too. Yes, her mother must have guessed something.

She said slowly, 'Mother took me to lunch at the Capriole. I was upset, and she insisted on shopping. You were there with Lizbeth. I—overheard a bit. I thought——' she cleared her throat '—I mean, it sounded as if she was trying to make you choose between us. And you—didn't think I could manage without you. Mother hurried me out of there as if she already *knew* . . .' Her voice became suspended. She knuckled her eyes.

'Oh, love,' said Justin, and took her hands in both of his. 'Don't cry. It's not what you think. Honestly. And I should've told you, only I knew you were upset, and I wanted to sort it out without your getting hurt if I could.' He put his arm round her and pulled her close. 'Lizbeth was wretched. But not over me. She isn't my girlfriend,' he said into her hair. 'I'm afraid she's your father's.'

Candy went rigid. It was so far from what she expected that he might have been speaking a foreign language.

'But she'd stayed with you at the flat. She started nest-building. Jeremy said,' she blurted.

Justin shook his head. 'She's a colleague. A trusted colleague. She's stayed overnight a couple of times when there's been a crisis. So have the other editors. She might have shoved the furniture about a bit. She's an assertive woman, and she fancies her interior decorating skills. But we were never lovers. Apart from anything else, I keep my private life out of the office.'

'I came to your office,' Candy murmured.

He shrugged. 'So that was another rule I broke for you. There've been plenty, God knows.'

'Oh,' said Candy. A thought occurred to her. 'So she was telling you about her affair with my father in that restaurant?'

Justin looked uncomfortable. 'Another broken rule, I'm afraid.'

'Why? How?'

'My staff's private life is their own affair. I've never interfered before. Lizbeth couldn't believe it. But she was at the end of her tether, and needed to talk, and I——' He flushed faintly.

'Yes?' asked Candy.

'You were so damned miserable,' he said in an uneven voice. 'Your parents were tearing you to pieces. I'd have done anything to stop it. None of my principles mattered a damn. I'd even have offered to buy Lizbeth off, if I thought it would do any good.'

He would have hated that. He must have hated the whole business.

He sent her a quick look. 'It wouldn't have been any use. Nothing would have changed it.' He looked compassionate suddenly, and his voice gentled. 'I've talked to your father. I'm afraid this time it's for real.'

Candy shook her head, trying to take it in. 'You did that for *me*?'

'Perverse, I know,' he said drily. He looked away. 'But there was nothing I could do. You'll have to be brave.'

He looked defeated. Candy could not bear it. She took his hands.

'I knew it would have to come to this eventually,' she said at last, with a sigh.

Justin's hands tightened. He looked startled. Candy drew a long breath, meeting that look.

'It's not my responsibility,' she went on steadily. 'I see that now. I told my mother this morning. It's her life. It's her problem. She's been making me a fifth wheel for too long.'

There was a stunned silence.

Justin said blankly, 'You mean I've been jumping through hoops trying to get that tedious pair together again, and you don't even *care*?'

Candy shook her head. 'Not much,' she told him, surprised. 'Not the way I care about us. Now that *is* my responsibility, rather than messing about with my parents' lives. And I haven't done very well by you so far. Have I?'

Justin's expression was arrested. He seemed to be monitoring himself rigorously. He asked gently, choosing his words with care, 'Are you sure? This isn't just shock, is it?' Candy shook her head vigorously. He went on in that same careful voice, 'You've always been so involved with them. The Centre too, I suppose. But mainly your parents. You're such a caring girl. But you didn't seem to have any room or time in your heart left for us. You and me.'

Just for a moment Candy glimpsed the bleakness.

'I thought if there was a solution for them—you might just start to give us a chance.' He sighed. 'I know Lizbeth. She's a tough lady and her career's important to her. I offered her an editorship in the States.'

He would have been so ashamed, Candy thought.

'Oh, *Justin.*'

He gave a twisted smile. 'She turned me down flat. Said she was in love. She said I ought to understand that even if I didn't understand anything else. They're going to get married. So it was all for nothing.'

He looked tired. For her he had broken all his rules, and it must seem to him now that he had behaved badly and stupidly. Candy wanted very much to take him in her arms. Looking at the defeated set to his mouth, she was suddenly full of anger.

She said crisply, 'Then my mother will either have to get used to living on her own or marry George Silk.

That's what he's wanted for years. She should never have married my father or used me as a sticking plaster to keep the marriage together.'

Justin looked at her, his expression weary. 'Don't lie to me, Candy,' he told her softly. 'When you first came to me about that story on your mother's gambling debts you were willing to put your whole life in pawn to keep them together.' He closed his eyes. 'That's why you married me,' he said almost to himself.

'That's not true.'

Incredulous, his eyes flew open. Meeting them, Candy shook her head violently.

'*No.* I was desperate to get away from them. I knew that unless I did it would never stop. But I wasn't trained for anything, and Dave didn't want me——' She bit it off. But it was too late.

'Ah,' said Justin. 'The second of life's mysteries answered. I wondered. So you married me because David Tresilian didn't want you.'

Candy would have given anything in the world to deny it. But she knew that this was a watershed, and she couldn't afford to lie now, not even by omission.

'In a way,' she admitted miserably at last. 'Now I re-alise that I didn't really know him. It was just a fantasy. Sometimes it was very lonely before I went to the Centre; and he was kind. When you and I first met I still— wanted that kindness to be more. Only to begin with, though,' she ended on a rush of painful honesty.

There was one of Justin's long silences. Candy could not look at him.

At last he said very softly, 'And to end with?'

'You mean now?'

He nodded. Candy took a deep breath and shut her eyes.

'I'm in love with you,' she said rapidly. 'I'm very sorry and I'll try not to be a nuisance——'

It was a sentence she was not destined to finish.

Justin took her in his arms and kissed her with a fervour bordering on savagery. There was no doubt about his feelings now. His expression was stripped to the bone. Candy could see—at least when he let her open her eyes and breathe again—all the pent-up doubts and repressed hope he had been harbouring. It was so like what she had been feeling herself that she put up a hand to his cheek and caressed it without any of that deadly self-consciousness.

Justin caught her hand and carried it to his mouth, turning it over so that he could press a kiss against the palm.

'Never stop being a nuisance,' he told her fervently.

She reached up and brought his head down to her, kissing him shyly but very openly.

'I've been so stupid.'

'Maybe a little,' he agreed on a breathless little laugh against her lips. The laugh deepened into a chuckle. 'Do you remember you once promised me no provocation? It made my blood run cold. It sounded like your mother talking to your father. And of course every damned thing you did was a provocation. I used to watch you climbing into that filthy old jacket to go to the Centre and break into a cold sweat with wanting to pull you back and make love to you.' He rubbed his cheek against her hair. 'Will you ever forgive me? I wasn't really sour about the Centre. I know you do good work there. I was just eaten up with jealousy of Tresilian.'

Candy said quietly, 'There's no need. For a while I thought he was wonderful. In his own way he is, I suppose. I admire what he's doing. I was such a *child*. And he used to tease me, call me "love"—I built it up into a fairy-tale, but there was never any substance to it. In my heart of hearts, I knew it.'

Justin looked at her searchingly. 'So it *wasn't* Tresilian who frightened you so?'

Candy was astonished. 'No, of course not. I'd never have gone back to the Centre if he had.'

'That's why I thought it was so hopeless,' Justin murmured. 'Because I thought he'd scared you and you still kept going back. Who was it, then?'

'A man called Langton,' she revealed with difficulty. She hung her head. 'I felt an awful fool about that. His parents were friends of Pops'.'

'Tom Langton?'

She nodded.

'I know him too,' Justin said grimly. 'Thick and noisy. I can see you wouldn't have cared for it.'

'I didn't care for the appetite he had for a rich wife, either,' Candy said drily. 'Oh, he scared me all right, but that wasn't the worst, Justin. He made me feel like part of a deal—a negligible part.'

'So Tresilian—who didn't scare you and made you feel as if you were doing a good job—scooped you on the rebound,' Justin said thoughtfully.

She flushed. 'Only up to a point.'

He looked at her searchingly. 'You're sure?'

'I'm sure. I wouldn't have been spending so much time at the Centre recently if—well, if you'd wanted to spend any time with me,' she told him. 'Dave wasn't the attraction. It's just that I seemed to be of some use there, and I wasn't needed at home.'

Justin said remorsefully, 'Negligible again, in fact. That was my fault, my darling. Things hadn't gone as I'd planned in France. I shouldn't really have gone away then, and although I'd made sure we wouldn't be interrupted I didn't have my whole concentration on you. Your father was doing some nasty deals behind my back.'

Candy frowned. 'I was afraid of that.' She looked at him candidly. 'I was afraid you blamed me at one time.'

His arm tightened.

She blushed a little but went on, 'Has he done something dreadful?'

Justin shrugged. 'Nothing I can't handle. But it all took time. And I'd thought you and I would have ourselves sorted out by the time we got back from the cottage. We hadn't, and I had to catch up with all the things I'd put off to go there in the first place. My secretary,' he added gloomily, 'said you'd leave me.'

Candy said shyly, 'You mean that, even before we went to France, you *wanted* to be married to me? That it wasn't a matter of convenience to you by then?'

Justin sighed. 'My darling, I lied to you. It was never a matter of convenience to me. I fell in love with you the moment I saw you.'

Candy said, '*What*?'

He made a face. 'I know. Pretty dubious behaviour for a tough businessman.'

She shook her head disbelievingly. Justin had the grace to look confused. He ran his hand through his hair.

'Look, I saw you at that party. So beautiful and scared to death. I just wanted to take you away somewhere. I wanted to make you happy, to make you laugh. I'd never reacted like that to anyone before. And then I found out who you were. I knew I had to be out of my mind. Then we talked and danced—and you were so *polite*. I kept thinking I was out with a china statue. Yet I had the feeling there was something more. And then you kissed me. Do you remember? There you were with your red hair all over the place, and I thought, This one's for me.'

Candy was blushing furiously. She shouted, 'Then why didn't you *say* so?'

Justin stroked his cheek against her hair. 'My darling, it would have frightened you witless. I may be a gambler but I'm not an idiot. I knew I had to bring you to it gently. Of course,' he added wryly, 'I could see you were going to be hell on wheels.'

It's not going to be easy. He had said it, and it had come back to haunt her that very evening. Perhaps she too had recognised the feeling, even though she didn't realise at the time.

She said, 'I've been very stupid. I didn't think anyone like you could possibly be interested. You even called me a schoolgirl.'

Justin's arms tightened. 'Pure frustration.'

She said shyly, 'I didn't think I was in your league, you know. It wasn't just Lizbeth Lamont. There was your first wife. And I'd never had a proper relationship—just a lot of silly fantasies about Dave. I didn't know how to judge where I stood with you. I remember thinking once—when you told me about Marianne—that I could leave you and it wouldn't even ripple the surface of your life. You're so self-contained. You don't seem to need anyone.'

He made an inarticulate protest and turned her face up to his. When they drew apart, their breathing was tortured. Candy's head swam.

'Withdraw that,' Justin told her, amusement flickering in the uneven tones.

Candy felt a sudden glorious sense of freedom. She could feel his smile like sunlight warming her through to her bones. She chuckled, drawing his head down to her and feathering a kiss across his lips.

'I do, I do,' she assured him. 'I'm a reformed character.' Justin held her away from him, looking dubious. 'I am,' she insisted. 'I'd even got some time off from the Centre *before* you turned up and started shouting at people this afternoon. I'm going to spend the next three weeks with you, wherever you are, working out exactly what constitutes provocation.'

She slid her hands under his jacket and began to slip open the buttons of his shirt. She felt his immediate reaction, and smiled to herself. Justin looked down at her, amused and so much more than amused.

One eyebrow rose. 'And then?' he asked at his most silky.

'And then,' said Candy with composure, reaching up to kiss his throat and loosen his tie at the same time, 'I'm going to make sure you get as much of it as you can stand for as long as we live.'

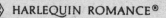

HARLEQUIN ROMANCE®

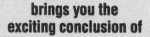

**brings you the
exciting conclusion of**

THE BRIDAL COLLECTION

next month with

THE REAL McCOY
by Patricia Knoll

THE BRIDE ran away.
THE GROOM ran after her.
THEIR MARRIAGE was over. *Or was it?*

Available this month in
The Bridal Collection
TEMPORARY ARRANGEMENT
by Shannon Waverly
Harlequin Romance #3259

WED-FINAL

HARLEQUIN ROMANCE®

welcomes you

BACK TO THE RANCH

Let your favorite Romance authors take you West!

Authors like Susan Fox, Debbie Macomber, Roz Denny, Rebecca Winters and more!

Let them introduce you to wonderful women and strong, sexy men—the men of the West. Ranchers and horsemen and cowboys and lawmen...

Beginning in June 1993

Wherever Harlequin books are sold.

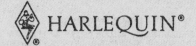 **HARLEQUIN®**

THE TAGGARTS OF TEXAS!

Harlequin's Ruth Jean Dale brings you
THE TAGGARTS OF TEXAS!

Those Taggart men—strong, sexy and hard to resist...

You've met Jesse James Taggart in FIREWORKS!
Harlequin Romance #3205 (July 1992)

And Trey Smith—he's THE RED-BLOODED YANKEE!
Harlequin Temptation #413 (October 1992)

And the unforgettable Daniel Boone Taggart in SHOWDOWN!
Harlequin Romance #3242 (January 1993)

Now meet Boone Smith and the Taggarts who started it all—
in LEGEND!
Harlequin Historical #168 (April 1993)

Read all the Taggart romances!
Meet all the Taggart men!

Available wherever Harlequin Books are sold.